"What happened, ___. ___ How did Tina Vale die?"

"Not sure," Jane answered. "Maybe suicide, maybe not."

"But *how* did she die?"

"Toaster fell in the bathtub, electrocuted her."

"How awful."

"She collected antique toasters."

"If she collected them, wouldn't she have known not to use one near water?"

"You'd think so."

"What are you saying, missus?"

Jane turned to face Florence. "Stanley thinks it may not have been suicide. There was a note, supposedly in Tina's handwriting, but it could have been faked. She said she couldn't go on. Why not? Everything was going well in her life."

"Then—"

"Stanley thinks it could have been murder. Because a key went missing. Someone in the suite between early this morning and the time Tina died grabbed that key and used it later to slip back in and kill her . . ."

Books by Evan Marshall

MISSING MARLENE

HANGING HANNAH

STABBING STEPHANIE

ICING IVY

TOASTING TINA

CRUSHING CRYSTAL

Published by Kensington Publishing Corporation

A Jane Stuart and Winky Mystery

TOASTING TINA

EVAN MARSHALL

KENSINGTON BOOKS
KENSINGTON PUBLISHING CORP.
http://www.kensingtonbooks.com

First Hardcover Printing: November 2003
First Mass Market Paperback Printing: October 2004
10 9 8 7 6 5 4 3 2 1

Printed in the United States of America

To my father,
Ronald Marshall,
with love

Acknowledgments

Thanks and appreciation to:

Joe Bajek, for explaining the ins and outs of electrocution with small appliances and thus helping me toast Tina.

John Scognamiglio, my editor, for his continuing support and encouragement.

Maureen Walters, my agent, for her wisdom and guidance.

My family and friends, for always being there.

For the poison of hatred seated near the heart doubles the burden for the one who suffers the disease; he is burdened with his own sorrow, and groans on seeing another's happiness.

—Aeschylus

Chapter One

Jane sat in the lobby of the Windmere Hotel and watched the entrance for someone who looked like a Nathaniel Barre. It was nearly 10:30. His plane was supposed to have landed in Newark at 9:20. According to Jane's calculations, he should arrive in Shady Hills any time now.

She'd told him to look for a tallish middle-aged woman (well, she *was* forty now) with shoulder-length auburn hair. He'd described himself only as having a mustache.

Car after car pulled up under the hotel's portico, but all the men who entered the building were cleanshaven. Jane took a handkerchief from her purse and dabbed at her forehead. Even in the air-conditioned lobby she could feel the July heat, or was she sweating because she didn't feel right about any of this, not right at all?

In all her years as a literary agent, Jane had never talked business in front of her clients. She felt it wasn't professional, wasn't appropriate. Tak-

ing care of business matters was *her* job; that's why
writers hired her, why they paid her a 15-percent
commission.

But Nathaniel Barre had insisted on flying in
from Green Bay, Wisconsin, for this meeting, and
for whatever reason, Jane hadn't had the guts to
tell him no.

She supposed it was because under the circumstances, she would probably have wanted to come
to the meeting, too. After all, she had sold Nat's novel,
The Blue Palindrome, for $900,000—more money,
he'd told her, than he'd expected to see in his
whole lifetime. Hamilton Kiels, the editor at Corsair Publishing who had bought the book in a
heated auction, said it was the most exciting acqui-
sition of his career. The company had huge plans
for this book and its author.

And then everything went wrong. One month
ago, Ham Kiels left Corsair to follow his editor-in-
chief, Jack Layton, to Penguin Putnam. Suddenly
Nat had no editor. Then it was announced that
Jack Layton would be replaced by Tina Vale, most
recently vice president and editor-in-chief of a
scrappy, avant-garde publisher called Bleecker
Books. Tina would have a higher title than Jack
had had: vice president and publisher.

When Jane heard this news, she felt a deadly
chill run through her. Tina Vale was one of the
most hated people in publishing—cold-blooded,
ruthless, manipulative, and cruel. And that was on
her good days.

The day after Tina arrived at Corsair, she phoned
Jane. Tina had found and read the manuscript Nat
had recently revised according to Ham Kiels' di-
rections, and the book had "major problems"—

words that inevitably shoot arrows of fear into an agent's heart. The bottom line was that Tina was rejecting the book.

A yellow taxi pulled up in front of the hotel and a man got out. Jane rose a little in her chair to see him. He was of medium height, portly, with too much dark hair and a bushy walrus mustache. The driver took from the trunk an ochre-colored, hard-sided Samsonite suitcase that looked as if it had been bought thirty years ago. The mustached man took it, handed the driver some bills, and headed into the hotel. Jane saw now that he wore a heavy tweed sport jacket that would have been perfectly appropriate in December, but on this 95-degree summer morning it made him look like a gauche out-of-towner, which she supposed he was.

For this had to be Nathaniel Barre, Jane's discovery, the anonymous pharmacist turned brilliant new novelist. He stopped inside the entrance and let his gaze travel around the vast jungle-like lobby. Jane rose and waved to him. He saw her but didn't smile, only nodded solemnly, picked up his suitcase, and made his way over to her.

"You're Nat," Jane said graciously, taking his wet, meaty hand. "Such a pleasure to meet you at last. I'm sorry it's under these circumstances."

"Well—mm," he said, nodding, and Jane realized she'd have to take charge. "Let me buy you a cup of coffee—we're still a little early for our meeting. There's a lovely café right over there."

He looked alarmed. "I'd better check in first, shouldn't I?"

"Yes, sure, of course." She changed direction and led him to the reception desk, watching as he spoke to one of the clerks. With the fuzzy tan tweed jacket he wore black slacks that looked as if they were pure polyester. Not the new, fashionable polyester, but polyester from the seventies. The pants' crotch hung low and the seat sagged. Jane's heart went out to this man whose unexpected talent had gained him a fortune he now stood an excellent chance of losing.

No wonder he'd wanted to fly out for this meeting with Tina Vale. At first, Tina had refused to meet with Jane at all, claiming she was too busy with her new responsibilities at Corsair. But Jane was determined to try to save this situation. For one thing, it was a terrible blow to the barely begun career of an exceptionally talented new writer. On a more practical level, he'd already bought himself and his mother, who lived with him (or did he live with her?) a massive new house. Worst of all, it was a blow to Jane's pocketbook: She had counted on earning a commission of $135,000 on Nat's $900,000 advance.

The day after Tina refused to see Jane, Jane read in *Publishers Weekly* that Tina would be coming to Shady Hills in three weeks to receive a Lifetime Achievement Award from Romance Authors Together (RAT), the country's leading romance writers' organization, which would be holding its annual conference, providentially, here at the Windmere Hotel. Jane immediately called Tina and asked to meet with her while she was in town. Grudgingly, Tina agreed. Jane would go to Tina's suite at eleven o'clock the first morning of the conference to "talk things over," though Tina warned Jane that her decision was final.

Coincidentally, Nat called Jane later that day to

find out if Corsair had accepted his revised manuscript, and if so, when he would receive the second third of his advance, due on acceptance of revisions.

Jane, never one to mince words, gave Nat all the bad news, mentioning her scheduled meeting with Tina. Nat was very quiet; then he abruptly announced, "I'm coming, too," and hung up.

Why hadn't she told him no? It occurred to her now that maybe she'd felt having the author actually there—making Tina look him in the eye—might make her change her mind. Had Jane made a terrible mistake?

Mistake or not, he was here now, stolidly thanking the clerk and carefully slipping his room key into his breast pocket as he lugged his suitcase back over to Jane.

"Now," she said cheerfully, "how about that coffee?"

"Is there really time?" He looked concerned. "I wouldn't want us to be late for the meeting."

She checked her watch; it was ten minutes to eleven. "I suppose you're right. I wanted to go over things first."

"Go over things?"

"Yes, you know—coach you a bit."

"Coach me?" He looked baffled. "What is there to coach me about? We're going up there to talk her out of rejecting my book, right?"

"Yes, I guess that pretty much sums it up." Taking a deep breath, she led the way to a house phone at the end of the reception desk. She asked for Tina's suite and when connected was told by a young woman to come up to Penthouse B.

They crossed the lobby toward a bank of elevators at the back. Passing the entrance to a large ballroom, they saw long rows of tables and men and women rushing about, many of them holding pet carriers. Nat frowned in puzzlement.

"That's the cat show," Jane said. "It starts today. My son and his nanny are entering our cat in the show—they'll be here around noon."

Nat peered into the room with interest. "You have a show cat?"

She laughed. "No, Winky is a just a good old domestic shorthair. A sweet little tortoiseshell. Nick and Florence are entering her in the Household Pet class."

"I see."

A wave of anxiety took hold of Jane. The cat show was the last thing she needed right now, with such a big piece of business in the balance. But Nick and Florence had been excitedly preparing for this event for weeks. Jane determined to put on her best face and muster up some enthusiasm. The plan was that after her meeting with Tina, Jane would remain at the romance convention, which she often attended because of the large number of romance writers she represented. When Winky was about to be judged, Florence would call Jane on her cell phone, and Jane would leave the convention long enough to hurry to the cat show to watch Winky compete.

Alone with Nat in the elevator, Jane smiled and glanced at him periodically as they began to rise to the penthouse floor. His forehead was beaded with sweat. "Would you be more comfortable if you took off your jacket?" she asked pleasantly.

He looked at her as if she'd suggested he remove his pants. "I'm fine, thank you." His brow creased in thought. "I've heard about this Tina Vale. They say she's . . . well . . . a tough cookie."

So he did have an idea of what he was in for. She laughed. "To say the least! Actually," she said, turning serious, "she's a monster. I don't think anyone in publishing is hated more than Tina Vale."

"Really? Even more than that woman at NAL?"

Jane threw back her head and laughed. She knew who he meant. "My, you *have* been doing your homework. Yes, even more." *And I should know.*

There were only two suites on the penthouse floor. At the door of Penthouse B they were greeted by a slim young woman in her late twenties. She had long, straight brown hair parted at the side and pretty pale-green eyes. For some reason, she looked familiar to Jane, as if she had met her before. But when she introduced herself as Shelly Adams, Jane decided she must be imagining things, because she had never met anyone by that name.

"Tina's in here." Shelly's tone was polite, pleasant. She showed them into a spacious living room furnished with contemporary pieces in cream, metal, and glass. Two entire walls provided views of Shady Hills—treetops rustling gently in the hot wind, large homes peeking through the leaves, the open oval of the village green, the bright white spire of St. John's Episcopal Church.

On a sofa to the left sat Tina herself, nestled into the pillows like a queen. She hadn't changed much, Jane thought. She was still beautiful—a blond ice maiden, like some modern-day Grace Kelly—though she looked tougher, even harder-edged, if that was possible, since Jane had last seen her. Their gazes met, and in Tina's silver-blue eyes Jane recognized undisguised loathing.

"Hello," Tina said coolly, sitting up a little, and glanced at the sofa on the other side of the coffee table. "Sit."

Jane didn't bother putting out her hand to the other woman. But she realized she should introduce Nat. "Tina Vale, I'd like you to meet—"

"I know who he is." Tina turned to Shelly, who hovered nearby. "Get me a cigarette."

Shelly turned, grabbed a cigarette from a holder on the bar behind her, and handed it to Tina.

"What am I supposed to light it with?" Tina snapped.

Just open your mouth and breathe some fire, Jane thought, and suppressed a nervous inward giggle.

Shelly found a lighter on the bar and lit Tina's cigarette. Tina inhaled deeply and, turning to Jane, blew out a thick cloud of smoke. "So. You're here. What did you want to say to me that you haven't already said?"

"Tina," began Jane, who had sat down beside Nat, and took a breath, "I want you to please rethink this. Give the novel to one of your editors, get another opinion. When I auctioned it, editors all over New York loved it. It's a brilliant piece of work. It's—"

"Shit! It's shit!" Tina said, looking right at Nat as if to make absolutely sure he knew she was insulting him. She turned to Jane with a scornful look. "I don't need anyone else's opinion. Do you think I got where I am by listening to what other people think? I tell *other* people what to think. And I'm telling you . . ." At this point she shifted on the sofa to face the coffee table, on which sat a manuscript whose title page bore the words *The Blue Palindrome.* "This"—she picked it up, holding it several feet above the floor—"is absolute garbage." And she let go. Pages flew everywhere, a flurry of white covered with hundreds of thousands of words.

Jane turned in alarm to Nat. She'd made a terrible mistake letting him come to this meeting. His jaw had dropped and he sat forward, his eyes bulging in disbelief.

Shelly gasped and hurried around the sofa, bending to pick up the pages.

"Stop it!" Tina shouted. "Get out of here!"

Shelly looked up at her, hurt on her pretty face, then dropped the pages and ran from the room.

Tina turned to Nat again, resting an elbow on her knee and cupping her chin in her hand. "You're a what?" she said with a pitying little smile. "A pharmacist?" She gave a little chuckle. "Let me tell you something, Mr. Best Dressed. You've got no business writing. Do you hear me? No business. If you're smart, you'll go back to pushing pills."

Jane, horrified by everything she had just witnessed, jumped up. "How dare you! You unspeakably rude monster. I will not allow you to speak to my client that way."

Tina drew back in feigned fear. "Ooh, the big agent gets tough." She puffed on her cigarette. "I remember that game. We used to play it together, remember? Put on a good show, make it look as if you're fighting hard for your client—even though you know you haven't got a snowball's chance in hell of getting your way. And you haven't, Jane. So why don't you and Mr. Deeds toddle on home?"

Nat jumped up and hurried toward the bed-rooms, presumably to go to the bathroom, proba-bly to be sick, Jane thought. For a long moment she simply stared at Tina, at a loss as to what to say.

"Tina," she finally began, "what is going on here? You don't like his manuscript and you're not going to change your mind—that's fine—but to behave this way . . . to insult him like that, unnec-essarily . . ." She narrowed her eyes shrewdly as Nat returned and took his seat beside her. "There's more to this than his manuscript, isn't there?"

Again Tina gave a little smile, but there was tri-umph in this one. "Damn right," she said, sud-denly slurring her words, and Jane realized she must have been drinking. That helped explain this bizarre behavior. "There's definitely more to this than his manuscript—which, by the way, I haven't even read."

"Well, what is it?" Jane demanded.

"It's simple. I hate you."

"*Hate* me? Why? What have I ever done to you?"

Tina shook her head. "You poor idiot. You've never known, have you? You took Kenneth away from me!"

Jane, a widow since her wonderful husband, Kenneth, had been killed by a truck four years ear-lier, sat for a moment in shocked silence. She tried to speak but could only shake her head to show her lack of comprehension.

"Okay," Tina said, "let me put you out of your misery. It amazes me you don't know this. I'll take you back a while—seventeen years, to be exact.

You and I were both at Silver and Payne, that bastion among literary agencies, and working alongside us was the most beautiful man I'd ever laid eyes on. Kenneth Stuart. You must have thought he was pretty dishy, too, because it didn't take you long to start screwing him."

"I loved him," Jane said quietly.

"Loved him," Tina spat. "Why? Because you were his assistant and he was nice to you? Explained contract language to you? Let you join him for lunch once in a while?" She leaned forward and stubbed out her cigarette on the glass coffee table. There was a crunchy sizzle. "Let me tell you something, sweetheart—something you never knew. When Kenneth climbed into your bed for the first time, he'd just climbed out of mine."

"I don't—"

"We'd been having an affair! For months! And guess what? It was a continuation of an affair we'd had ten years earlier. Surprise!"

"I never knew," Jane said softly, feeling faint.

"Obviously. But it's true." Tina's face filled with hatred. "*I* wanted him back, but he left me for you. Said he was in love with you. Trouble was, *I* loved *him*. First time that had ever happened to me—me loving someone. It's never happened again."

Beside Jane, Nat shifted uncomfortably on the sofa and she turned to look at him. He was sweating heavily again and his eyes stared out from under his bushy brows in alarm. Suddenly he jumped up and started for the door.

"Oh, wait!" Tina said, and he froze. "I have something for you." She picked up a piece of paper from the coffee table and handed it to Jane. It was a sheet of Corsair Publishing letterhead, with the words TINA VALE, VICE PRESIDENT AND PUBLISHER printed at the top. On it was a note, scrawled in Tina's trademark sloppy handwriting. Jane's gaze lighted on a few lines in the middle:

> *I'm terribly sorry, but I can't go on with this pro-ject. The manuscript as revised is still unacceptable, and we do not feel that it would be in either our or Mr. Barre's best interest for us to publish it . . .*

"First thing Monday morning," Tina said, "I'm going to tell our legal department to send you a contract termination document." She pointed to the letter and smiled. "That's something for you to enjoy in the meantime, Pill Man."

Nat grabbed the letter from Jane's hand and stormed out of the suite, slamming the door behind him.

"Hey," Tina said with a shrug. "He wanted to come to this meeting. Poor slob didn't know how much we had to talk about."

"You're a liar," Jane said.

"A liar? What am I lying about?"

"Kenneth."

Tina laughed. "Can't take the truth?" She smiled a sly drunken smile and her gaze shifted sideways as she remembered. "I used to love the way Kenneth would hold his breath just before he cli-maxed, then let it out in a sudden whoosh. And do you remember that darling tiny mole he had right near the end of his—"

"Stop it!" Tears threatened the corners of Jane's eyes but she fought them back. She pulled herself together as best she could. "What," she asked quietly, "does your hating me for taking Kenneth away from you have to do with Nat Barre's manuscript?"

"Nothing! It's just that this is the first opportunity I've had to get revenge, to hurt you back. I knew I'd have the chance someday. Your author is simply—what was that marvelous term Timothy McVeigh used?—collateral damage."

"You won't get away with this. I'll go over your head. I'll talk to Rafe Parker," Jane said, referring to Corsair Publishing's chairman of the board. "I'll tell him everything you've said today."

"Be my guest," Tina said. "I'm screwing him. Whose side do you think he'll take? No one at Corsair will take your side over mine. If I say *The Red Lollipop* or whatever the hell the book is called is dreck, it's dreck."

There was a sound from another room and a man appeared from the hallway leading to the bedrooms. Of medium height and slender, he had good-looking, refined features and dirty blond hair that curled attractively at the collar of his open-neck white shirt.

Tina half-turned. "Ah, Ian, I didn't know you were here."

He smiled. "I just came back." The suite must have had a second entrance, Jane realized. Ian came farther into the room and Jane could see that he was carrying something. Strangely, it looked like an old toaster. He walked up behind Tina on the sofa and bent to plant a chaste kiss on her forehead. "I found you something," he teased in a singsong voice.

"You did?" Suddenly Tina was like a little girl.

"Mm-hm." Ian brought the toaster up over her

head and placed it on her lap. "It's a . . . Toast-O-Lator!"

Tina squealed with delight. "You're kidding?" She turned to Jane with an energetic smile, as if their entire meeting had never taken place. "I've been looking for one of these for years." She held it out for Jane to see. "You see, it walks the bread through on a conveyer belt at the bottom of the slot. Isn't it darling?"

This woman must be mad. Jane rose.

"Oh, hello," Ian said, noticing her for the first time.

"Hello," Jane replied coldly.

"And you are . . . ?"

"Jane Stuart," Tina said. "She's an agent." She might have been saying "leper."

Ian was clearly uninterested in either Jane or what she did for a living. He immediately returned his attention to Tina and the toaster. "You like?"

Jane cleared her throat commandingly. Ian turned to her.

"And you are . . . ?" she said to him coolly.

He blinked. "I'm Ian Stein. Tina's husband."

Tina said, "Wherever we go, I send him out on these toaster hunts. Oh, Ian, you've outdone yourself this time."

"Got it for a song, too," he said with a self-satisfied grin. "Old cow had no idea what she was selling me."

"That's the best news of all."

Jane could stand it no more. Tina's husband must have heard her say she was screwing Rafe Parker, but he didn't seem to care. Now they had turned into children playing with toasters.

She turned and walked out of the suite, nearly

colliding with Nat, who stood in the hall against the wall. "I felt I should wait for you," he said.

She felt her face flush with fury. "I've never thought I could commit murder—until now."

She heard a sound and turned. Shelly Adams peered out at them through a crack in the door to Tina's suite. She blinked twice, then quickly shut the door.

Chapter Two

——————

"I'm sorry, Nat," Jane said, pressing the elevator L button. "You shouldn't have had to hear those things."

"No, I'm sorry," he said, surprising her with his sudden sensitivity. "Sorry that she hurt you like that."

"Thanks," she said, and they rode a little in silence as the elevator slowly descended. "She's a monster, as you can see."

"I can't imagine what it would have been like to work with her."

"Fortunately she wasn't at Silver and Payne long."

"She quit?"

"Oh, no, it's much more interesting than that. A few months after she starting working at the agency, she began having an affair with Henry Silver, the old man who owned it. Once she was safely ensconced as Henry's mistress, she set herself up as a rival to Beryl Patrice, who ran the agency. Beryl had once had an affair with Henry herself, and had never gotten over him. Well, things between the two women got worse and worse until one day Beryl walked in on Tina sitting on Henry's lap, kissing him. Beryl went berserk. She had a drinking problem and was a bit tipsy at the time."

The elevator doors opened onto the lobby and they stepped out, Nat listening intently.

Jane went on, "Beryl stood in the middle of the offices and screamed at Tina—called her the worst kinds of names."

"What did Tina do?"

"She got up very calmly from Henry's lap, walked into Beryl's office, found a bottle of vodka Beryl had hidden at the back of one of her desk drawers, and poured it all out on Beryl's head. Then Tina walked out of the office and never came back. That was the last time I saw her . . . until today.

"The next day, Henry fired her. Tina retaliated by filing a wrongful dismissal lawsuit, which was ultimately settled, Tina receiving in excess of a million dollars.

"She became an editor after that. She worked for a bunch of publishers before Bleecker Books, the last place she worked before Corsair." Jane shook her head. "I've always managed to avoid her—until now."

Nat shook his head in wonder. "Wow. I never had any idea publishing was so . . . interesting."

"That kind of interesting I can do without," Jane said, and led the way over to two inviting-looking armchairs at the end of the lobby. "Let's sit a minute, figure out our game plan."

He obediently sat.

"There's no point in going over Tina's head," she said. "That much is clear. Rafe Parker would just refer it all back to Tina."

"And she's rejecting it without even having read it!"

"Right. It could be the best novel since *Gone With the Wind* and she would still reject it. No," she said thoughtfully, "we'll go to the underbidder in the auction. It was Gary Kostikian at St. Martin's."

"What about Hamilton Kiels and Jack Layton? They liked it enough to win the auction. Do you think they would want to publish it at Penguin Putnam?"

"Maybe. Not a bad idea, actually. We'll try both, for starters." She flipped out her cell phone, called the office, and left a message for Daniel when he came in on Monday, asking him to have half a dozen fresh copies of *The Blue Palindrome* made. She would explain everything.

"Well!" she said, looking around the bustling hotel. "There's not much more we can do at this point, short of a good stiff drink—and it's a bit early for me. Speaking of drinking, did you notice that Tina was slurring her words?"

"Yes, I did. She's clearly got a problem."

Jane shrugged. "Which is not my problem. Are you going back to Wisconsin today? There's no reason for you to stick around."

"I've decided not to go back yet," he said with sudden conviction. "I figure since I'm here, I might as well check out this romance convention that's going on. After all, most of my readers are women, right?"

"Most *readers* are women."

"Exactly! Which means most of my readers will

be women. I want to see how this whole women's fiction thing works. I might even stop in at the cat show. Mother and I have eight."

"Eight what?"

"Cats."

Jane had always privately believed that a person could have up to four cats and still be considered sane. Any more and you were a "crazy cat person." She gave Nat a long, considering look, then checked her watch. It was a few minutes before noon. Nick and Florence were due to arrive with Winky now. She rose, and so did Nat.

"Thanks for everything, Jane. For fighting for me, I mean. You're a great agent."

"Why, thank you, Nat," she said, truly touched, and gave him a warm smile. "I'll see you around the hotel, okay?"

"Definitely," he said, then looked up, remembering something. "You'll be pleased to hear that I've already started my second novel. Brought my laptop along to work on it. In fact, before I start checking out the convention, I'm going to visit the library to do some research. Can you tell me how to get there?"

"Of course. I think it's marvelous that you've already started your next book. It will certainly help take your mind off this mess. Just take Route 46 East and get off at Packer Road. You'll see the library on the left."

"Great. Thanks again, Jane."

"My pleasure." She watched him walk toward the hotel entrance. She realized she was still quite shaken up from her close encounter of the Tina kind. Perhaps just one drink wouldn't be a bad idea. At the side of the lobby opposite the reception desk was a restaurant called Tuscany Hills. She made her way around a small palm tree, already having narrowed her options down to a martini or a glass of white wine, when all at once an enormous obstacle loomed into her path.

She stopped short and looked up into the heavily pancaked face of a woman who appeared to be in her mid-sixties. Everything about her was massive. Easily six feet tall, she wore a shiny leopard-print muumuu that looked as if it had been fashioned from a bedspread. Making her look even bigger was a huge twirl of hair on the top of her head that looked like glossy black cotton candy. Jane was immediately reminded of the late actor Divine.

"Excuse me," Jane said, trying to get around this human roadblock, but it moved with her.

"Jane Stuart?" the woman said in a deep, booming voice.

Jane stopped short. "Yes?"

The woman waited, hands on hips, as if expecting Jane to recognize her.

"Uh . . . have we met?" Jane asked.

"I," the woman said grandly, "am Salomé Sutton."

Jane's jaw dropped. Salomé Sutton! Salomé Sutton was the undisputed queen of romance, credited with inventing the modern historical romance with her groundbreaking novel *Arabian Nights,* featuring the legendary Delilah Dare, the beautiful, headstrong princess abducted by the brooding Roan Romero disguised as a sheikh. It was said that all of the legendary writers of historical romance—Kathleen Woodiwiss, Rosemary Rogers, Jennifer Wilde—got their inspiration from Salomé

Sutton. Jane was twelve years old when she read *Arabian Nights,* and she had read every Salomé Sutton novel since.

Should she bow? Genuflect? "Oh, Miss Sutton, it is an honor to meet you. I've been a fan of yours for so many years. I can't believe I'm finally—"

"Listen, sweetie, cut the crap, okay? We gotta talk. You had lunch yet?"

"No, I haven't."

"Great. Come on." Salomé led the way farther into the quiet restaurant. Watching the older woman's wide bottom straining the muumuu from side to side, Jane wondered if she would end up representing this legend. It would be an agent's dream come true—not to mention ample compensation for the anguish she'd just been through in Tina Vale's suite.

On the way to a table, Jane glanced quickly at her watch and realized that Nick and Florence would probably have arrived by now. She'd just pop in and see how they were doing.

"Excuse me, Miss Sutton."

"Sal, call me Sal. That's what my friends call me."

"Excuse me, Sal, but I've got to check on something for a moment. May I meet you here?"

"Sure, no prob. You want me to order you something?"

"Yes, a martini, please."

Sal's big face broke into the sweetest of grins. "Now you're talkin'."

In the cat ballroom, Jane found Nick and Florence busily setting up Winky's cage on one of the tables the show had provided.

"Missus! Hello, hello," Florence said, never stopping her work. "How is your day going?"

"Bumpy so far, Florence. And you?"

Florence's pretty coffee-colored face lit up and she tilted her head toward Nick, who was on his knees, speaking to Winky in her carrier. "Our little mister is working very hard," Florence said, "but I've explained there's a lot of competition."

Both women let their gazes travel across the ballroom, a bustling sea of cat cages and their owners.

"Yeah, Mom, it's cat-eat-cat in here—get it!" Nick broke into a high-pitched giggle, and Jane ruffled his soft brown hair.

Florence took from a bag the burgundy velvet curtains Jane had sewn specially for this event and began draping them inside the cage. "They are perfect, missus."

"Good. Now listen. I'll be here in the hotel when it's time for Winky to go on. Just call my cell phone."

"Got it, Mom," Nick said, and as if to agree Winky let out a yowl so loud it drew the attention of people on both sides of them.

"Break a leg, Wink!" Jane said, and hurried back out to the lobby.

Salomé was on her second screwdriver when Jane arrived at the table. "Been wanting to meet you for years," she said as Jane sat down.

"Really? Why?"

"I been watchin' you. I like the way you work. I read a lot of the books you sell. I like your style."

"Thank you," Jane said. "It's a shame we've had to wait this long to meet."

"Mm. I guess I was afraid to make one wrong move when I was with my last agent."

"And who was that?"

"Mankewitz. You know him?"

"I don't know him personally, but I know *of* him, of course." Jory Mankewitz, of Mankewitz & Donnelly, was as legendary as Salomé, as prominent an agent today as Henry Silver had been twenty years earlier.

"You're . . . no longer with him?" Jane asked delicately.

"Right. Dumped the bastard."

Jane nearly choked on her martini. Offhandedly she asked, "Things, uh, weren't working out anymore?"

Sal slammed down her glass so hard that half her drink sloshed out onto the table. "Yeah, you could say that. But let me back up. Tina Vale—you know her?"

"Yes. Yes, I do."

"You know she's runnin' Corsair now, right?"

"Yes."

"And you know that up to now, I've been Corsair's biggest earner. Every June for years a new Salomé Sutton came out and kept that damn shop afloat. Even this year. You read *My Dark Desires*, came out last month?"

Jane had devoured it in three days. "I loved it," she breathed.

"Thanks, I'm glad." Sal patted Jane's hand. "Point is, this Tina comes in and suddenly things are different. Because Tina's got a pet of her own, this"—she struggled to remember the name— "Queen, that's it. Stephanie Queen. Now she's going to be their lead author, and I'm yesterday's oatmeal."

"But I'm sure they'll continue to publish you in a big way," Jane said.

Sal peered at her through squinting eyes. "You an agent, or Pollyanna? Get real! You think this Queen bitch is going to put up with them pushing me too? Queen's gonna be the queen, and that's that."

"So what are you going to do about it?"

"What am I going to do?" She grabbed up her menu, gave it a fierce glance, and tossed it aside. "Where the hell is the waiter? Waiter!" She returned her attention to Jane. "I'm going to get the hell out of Corsair, that's what I'm going to do about it. My career's going down the tubes; I see that already."

"Don't you think you're being a bit—um—hasty?"

"Hasty! Honey, if you think I'm being hasty, you don't know publishing, and you definitely don't know this Vale bitch. From what I hear, she's Cruella De Vil and Eva Braun rolled into one—plus she eats her young . . . if she has any."

"I don't believe she does."

"You know what I mean. She's an animal, a killer. She doesn't give a damn about me, a fat old broad who was already there when she arrived. She wants her own people, her own feathers in her cap. That's publishing, ain't it?"

"Yes," Jane agreed sadly, "lately, that's publishing. Then, are you moving to another publisher?"

"It's not that easy. A few weeks before Cruella arrived, I delivered the last book of my current contract. Soon as she got there, I knew I was doomed and told Jory to get the book back and get me out of there. You know what Cruella and her lawyer henchman said? No way, unless she wants to pay us twice what we've already paid her for it. Now that is really low. I told them so, adding that I'm not made of money. They said, 'In that case, we'll be very happy to publish the book as planned. We think it's splendid.' Splendid! The lawyer actually used that word. Weasel."

Jane was surprised that an agent as powerful as Jory Mankewitz had been unable to buy back Salomé's book. "Did Jory try again?"

"Nope. Refused. Said there was no use. So I fired the schmuck."

"Really?"

"Yup. Which is why I wanted to talk to you, sweetie pie."

The waiter finally arrived.

"Thought you went on vacation," Salomé said. "Gimme the chef's salad, extra Thousand Island dressing. And another screwdriver."

Jane ordered a salad, too.

When the waiter had gone, Salomé continued. "I want to make you a business proposition. I'll sign with your agency—for now."

"For now?"

"For now. You say you're representing me and try to get that book back from Corsair for the money they've paid me so far for it—I ain't got the acceptance money yet, obviously. If you can get it back on those terms, I'll sign with you permanently—I'll be your slave, your indentured servant—and you can sell that book, and all my future books, to another publisher. I've already got ideas about that, by the way. I think Warner's doing some really interesting things and that there's a place for me there. So, what do you think?"

Why was there always a catch? Jane wondered sourly. Why didn't big writers just come to her, with no strings attached?

Inwardly, she sighed. You had to take your opportunities as they came to you, and this was one she wasn't going to pass up. She'd try to get Salomé's book back, and if she succeeded, it would have been more than worth the effort. If she didn't, then she'd have gambled and lost.

"I'll do it," Jane said, breaking into a big smile and putting her hand on Sal's.

"Atta girl! I know you can do it. Good good good."

Over Salomé's shoulder, Jane noticed a group of people entering the restaurant. With a sick pang in her stomach she realized it was Tina Vale, Ian Stein, and Jory Mankewitz himself, looking exceptionally tall, slim, and suave in his trademark black Italian suit. Jane had never met Mankewitz, but everyone knew what he looked like.

Salomé followed Jane's gaze. "Well, if it ain't Cruella and her entourage." She threw Jory a nasty look.

"Now," Jane said cheerfully, trying to distract Salomé, "let's start with the name of the book you've just delivered."

"Huh?" Salomé's gaze was fixed on the three people taking seats at the other end of the restaurant. Tina, making her way to a seat against the wall, suddenly stumbled, and Ian caught her by the arm and steadied her.

Salomé shook her head. "She's got a problem with the bottle, that one. I went up to see her in her suite this morning, you know. I wanted her assurance that if she wouldn't let go of my book, she would give me the kind of publicity and promotion I've always had. She laughed at me, said no author was ever going to tell her how to do her job. Mean bitch—said I'd be lucky if I got a classified ad in the *Penny Saver*.

"Anyway, she was blitzed even then—early in the morning! Slurring her words, dropping things . . ."

"Now, what did you say the title of that novel is?"

"Mean and spiteful, that's what she is. And as for my agent, who worked so hard to try to get my book back for me, there he is, sleeping with the enemy! I'll bet he tried real hard, don't you think?"

Slowly, ponderously, like Gargantua appearing above a skyscraper, Salomé rose. She turned toward Tina, Ian, and Jory, who were laughing pleasantly at their table across the room, and started toward them.

Chapter Three

"Now, Sal..." Jane said, reaching out to her. But the older woman was already halfway across the restaurant. Tina and her party hadn't noticed her. A waiter approached her and said, "Can I get you something, ma'am?"

"Get out of my way!" she yelled, and Tina, Ian, and Jory looked up in surprise. Tina rolled her eyes and Jane heard her say, "Oh, for Pete's sake."

And then Salomé was upon them. *"You!"* she shrieked, grabbing Jory Mankewitz by the lapels and yanking him to his feet as if he were a little boy. "You wouldn't fight anymore to get my book back, and now I know why! Because you're sleeping with the enemy!" She began to shake Jory, whose eyes bugged out in horror.

"Call the police!" the waiter shouted to the restaurant's hostess, who rushed to her phone.

Ian had risen from his chair and was trying to pull Salomé off Jory. Salomé pushed him off like an elephant swatting a fly. Ian lost his balance and fell back into his chair.

"Help!" Tina cried.

A man ran into the restaurant, tall and sandy-haired, with exceptionally broad shoulders. He hurried up to the table, put his arms around Salomé, and somehow subdued her. "Where are you sitting?" Jane heard him ask her gently, and when he and Salomé turned, Jane realized that the man was Stanley—her very own boyfriend, Detective Stanley Greenberg—of the Shady Hills Police Department.

His arm around Salomé, he walked over to Jane's table and smiled. "Why, hello, Mrs. Stuart," he said, a twinkle in his eye.

"Detective Greenberg," she greeted him briskly.

He helped Salomé into her chair, one hand still on her ample upper arm. "Now, do you think you're okay? Because we really can't have this kind of behavior." He pulled over a chair from another table and straddled it, watching Salomé, waiting for an answer.

"I'm fine now," she said, and gave herself a little shake. "Just give me a sec to pull myself together."

Stanley winked at Jane.

"Anyway," Salomé said, "I don't need to dirty my hands fighting with trash like that. I've got Jane to fight for me now."

Stanley looked at Jane askance. "Is that so?"

"Sure is," Jane said proudly. "Detective Greenberg, allow me to introduce Salomé Sutton, the queen of romance—and my new client."

Stanley, always looking out for Jane's best interests, gave her a private lift of the eyebrows as if to say, "Money?" and she gave him a slow smiling nod in response, even though she wasn't so sure, not after the scene in Tina Vale's suite that morning.

"Anyhow," Salomé said, pushing away her untouched chef's salad, "I'm gonna run. I'm on a panel or something in a few minutes. She opened her black patent leather purse, pulled out a business card, and handed it to Jane. "There's my vital statistics. Call me anytime. And good luck." She rose. "Detective, it's been a pleasure to meet you." And she made her way between the tables, her great bulk pushing chairs away, until she reached the lobby and was out of sight.

Jane looked down at the card. Salomé lived in affluent Rancho Santa Fe, California. She commented on this to Stanley.

"I'm impressed," he said. "Is she really the queen of romance?"

"Actually, yes. It was her book, *Arabian Nights*, that started—"

"That's okay, Jane. I'll take your word for it."

She laughed. "She's my client, but with a catch. If I can accomplish what she wants, she'll be my biggest client. Now, what are you doing here?"

"Looking for you. We got a report about some bickering over in one of the conference rooms. I came to sort things out—though it's been quiet since I arrived. I knew you were coming to this thing and decided to try to find you. So—how did your morning go?"

She told him about her and Nat Barre's meeting with Tina Vale. Listening, he stared in amazement.

"And that blonde across the room," Jane finished, "is the lady herself."

"The gorgeous one? She doesn't look like a monster."

"They never do. You'll have to trust me on this one."

"That stinks. Sorry to hear it, Jane." He looked at her shrewdly. "But I think something else is bothering you. Or something more. Something you haven't told me yet. Did I get the whole story?"

She stared at him, marveling. "You know me too well." Suddenly she burst into tears.

"Jane," he said, putting his arm tightly around her, "what is it?"

Through her tears, she told him what Tina had said about Kenneth. "It's too awful," she finished. "Why didn't Kenneth ever tell me?"

"That's an easy one," Stanley said, giving her a sweet, gentle smile. "Because he didn't want to hurt you." There was love in Stanley's eyes, as if he fully understood Kenneth's thinking.

She rose up a little and kissed him on the cheek. "You are a good man, Stanley. Thank you. Now," she said, wiping at her tears with a tissue from her purse and pulling herself together. "What are you up to for the rest of the day?"

"Checking in on the cat show, for one thing."

"Oh, yes! I'll be getting a call when Winky's about to go on, or however they say it in cat shows."

He nodded, rising. "I'll be floating around. I understand these romance people can be troublesome. See you." He kissed her and left the restaurant.

Jane got down a bit of salad, but she wasn't very hungry. She took a few more bites, sipped at her water, and got up, making a point of not looking in the direction of Tina's table. She checked her watch. It was 1:30, and the romance convention's first round of workshops was about to begin.

Reaching the restaurant's entrance, she decided she couldn't take sitting in an audience full of cackling authors right now. She found a quiet place in the lobby's jungle area, a comfy forest-green padded armchair hidden among oversize palm fronds. She had just lowered herself into the delicious cool chair when she heard a soft voice say, "Mrs. Stuart?" and looked up.

It was Shelly Adams, Tina Vale's secretary. She stood before the chair in her prim gray skirt and white blouse, her hands clasped in front of her like a schoolgirl.

"I'm sorry to bother you," she said meekly, "but I wondered if I could talk to you. It's about what happened upstairs."

Chapter Four

"Yes, of course," Jane replied, puzzled. "Here," she said, and pulled over another armchair. Shelly lowered herself into it, the top part of her body perfectly erect.

"I hope you'll forgive me," Shelly said softly, "but I overheard the awful things Tina said to you. I wanted to tell you how sorry I am."

"Why, thank you. That's very kind."

"She's like that with everybody, me especially. I've been putting up with it for far too long. In fact," Shelly said, lifting her head proudly, "just before Tina and Ian went downstairs for lunch, I quit!"

"You quit?"

"Sure did. Gave two weeks' notice. Walked right up to her, told her I couldn't work for someone who treats people the way she does, and said she could take her job and . . . well, keep it."

Jane, taking an immediate liking to this sweet young woman, congratulated her.

"Thanks," Shelly said. "It was really long overdue. Those things she said to you this morning . . . I've heard her say a lot of horrible things to a lot of people, but I've never heard her say things as cruel as that. It was the last straw, as far as I was concerned."

"Well, thank you again," Jane said, and they both sat for a moment, silently, Jane sensing there was more Shelly wanted to say. She waited.

Finally Shelly said in a soft voice, "Can I tell you what Tina did to me?"

"Of course, if it will make you feel better."

"It will." Shelly moved forward a little in her chair, to get closer to Jane. "A few months ago, my boyfriend, Terry, and I got engaged."

"Congratulations."

"Yeah, thanks, but hold the congratulations. I'll tell you why in a minute. Terry and I had always talked about buying a little house, a place of our own. Terry actually had his eye on a place—a house in Fair Lawn, where he lives. Anyway, I told Tina about our engagement."

"And how did she react?"

"She was actually nice about it! Then came the shocker. When I told her we were going to buy a little place as soon as we could save the down payment, she offered to lend it to us, interest free!"

"That is a shocker."

"Yeah, well, it didn't happen. Several times I asked her—nicely, you know, because I didn't want to be pushy or seem greedy—when Terry and I could have the money. She always put me off—she wouldn't answer, or she'd change the subject, or she'd say something vague like 'Soon.'

"Two days ago, the owner of the house Terry

and I had our eye on told Terry that if we weren't going to buy it, he was going to sell it to someone else who had just made a bona fide offer."

"Did you tell this to Tina?"

"Yes, immediately. This time she acted as if I was crazy—as if she'd never offered to lend us the money. She yelled at me to stop bothering her with my 'pathetic little problems.' I know she must really have remembered her offer, though, because as I ran off crying I heard her say, 'Why should you be happy when I'm not?' "

Tears ran down Shelly's cheeks and she bit her lower lip between her teeth. "The worst part is that when I told Terry what had happened, we had a terrible fight. He said I had bungled it with Tina, that I should have handled it better so that we'd have gotten the money. He was so upset and ugly with me that I told him I didn't want to marry him anymore. And I don't," she said, looking earnestly into Jane's eyes. "I can't be with any more people who treat me like that."

"No, you certainly can't," Jane agreed stoutly, and put her arm around the young woman's shoulder.

Shelly sniffed. "Thanks. You're really nice, you know that? Anyway, all of this was by way of saying I know how it feels to be a victim of Tina's cruelty, and I'm really sorry about what happened."

"Thank you."

Shelly nodded, jumping up from her chair. "And now I guess I'm leaving. It feels weird—not to go back upstairs to finish my work, I mean."

"But it will also feel wonderful. Good luck."

Shelly practically curtsied, then turned and hurried off. Jane watched her hurry out of the hotel's entrance and speak to the doorman, who whistled for a cab.

At that moment there came the sound of voices raised in argument. Jane turned toward the noise and, peering around the trunk of a palm tree, realized it was coming from a conference room near the cat show ballroom.

A middle-aged woman in a dark suit was arguing with three women dressed in medieval gowns and headdresses. Jane figured the gowned women would be participating in a RAT convention favorite event, the Fashion of Passion Pageant, in which readers dressed up as their favorite romance-novel heroines.

Listening, Jane ascertained that the women were fighting over which group—the cat show or the RAT convention—had the right to use this room.

"Look at this!" cried one of the gowned women, who wore a pointy cone hat with a veil dangling from the tip, which Jane had learned from reading historical romances was called a henin. The woman waved a sheet of paper in the face of the woman in the dark suit. "This is a contract with the hotel saying we've got this room—Conference Room D!"

The woman in the suit was holding a sheet of paper as well. She snapped it in the face of the other woman. "Read this!" She jabbed hard at the paper with her finger. "Conference Room D!"

"But what's the date on yours? Ours is April 12th."

The woman in the suit started to look, then threw out her hands in exasperation. "I'm not going to argue with you about this." Wasn't that exactly what they were doing? Jane wondered. "If you don't get out of here, I'm calling the police."

Suddenly another of the gowned women—this one wearing a barbette-and-fillet hat—stomped forward and shoved the woman in the suit squarely in the chest, moving her backward a good two yards. "You just try it, baby, and I'll take those cats of yours and shove them right up your—"

"Ladies! Ladies!"

It was Stanley. Like magic, he had appeared in the doorway and now rushed in, separating the women.

"Who the hell are you?" the third gowned woman asked.

"Stanley Greenberg, detective, Shady Hills Police Department. We can't have fighting like this in the hotel."

"She started it," the first gowned woman whined, pointing at the woman in the suit.

A middle-aged man in a blue blazer and gray slacks hurried into the room. "Mrs. Bryant," he said to the woman in the suit, "I've already explained to you that there's a problem and that we'll work it out." He turned to Stanley. "I'm Andrew Cowan, the hotel manager. We made an error. We overbooked the hotel. This room has been reserved by both the cat show and the romance convention."

"Well," Stanley said equably, "who had it first?"

Cowan looked from Mrs. Bryant to the gowned women, as if afraid to answer. Finally he said, "I believe the RATs—I mean the romance convention's letter of agreement has the earlier date."

"There you are, then," Stanley said. "That means the second letter was invalid." He turned to Mrs. Bryant. "I'm sorry, ma'am. Maybe Mr. Cowan here can work something else out for you."

Good old Stanley, Jane thought; he always knew

what to do in difficult situations like that. She smiled, shaking her head in wonder.

Suddenly she was aware of someone standing behind her. "Tell me," came a man's silky voice in her ear, "do you make a habit of spying on people from behind palm trees?"

Chapter Five

Jane gasped and spun around. It was Jory Mankewitz. His face bore a kindly, paternal expression.

"I was just—" she began.

He laughed. It sounded like a velvet waterfall.
"I'm kidding you! I was finding it pretty fascinating
myself. But tell me—how can you tell the difference between the RATs and the cats?"

"Ooh, you're bad," Jane said, liking him already.

Abruptly his expression turned serious. "May I
speak with you?"

"You already are."

"Walk with me in the hotel gardens."

Intrigued, she followed him out of the jungle,
across the lobby, and out the hotel's rear door into
a large courtyard planted with shade trees and
vivid banks of yellow and red marigolds. A fountain played in the center. She stood gazing into the
water, certain he intended to reprimand her for
what she perceived as her poaching Salomé Sutton
from him.

He came up beside her. "Do you know Tina Vale?"

She slid him a wary glance. "Yes," she said slowly. "Why?"

"She's just burned me very badly. Come, let's walk." He led the way out of the courtyard onto the lawn, which sloped down to thick woods in the distance.

"No one knows this," he said, walking beside her, "but before Tina accepted her present job at Corsair, she and I had planned to start a company together—a literary agency."

She turned to him in surprise.

He nodded. "It's true. She'd told me she wanted to return to agenting, that it was her first love. We made a plan. We would both quit our jobs at the same time.

"So . . . as soon as I heard she had quit her job at Bleecker Books, I left Mankewitz & Donnelly, the firm I helped found. But Tina, I soon learned, had accepted a job at Corsair, without even telling me. She'd broken her word."

"That sounds like Tina."

He shook his head. "I'm a fool and deserve this, I suppose. I always knew what she was capable of, knew the kinds of horrible things she had done to other people. I thought how wonderful it would be to go into partnership with a woman like that, a woman as tough as that. It never occurred to me that I would be one of her victims.

"I wasn't going to give up on our idea, though. Not yet, at least. I'd already made plans to come to this convention to see some of my authors who were going to fly in from various parts of the country. Then I heard that Tina would be here. So I asked to see her, and to my surprise, she said yes.

"I went up to her suite this morning and confronted her in person for the first time since she went back on her word. When I asked her why she'd done what she had, she shrugged and said she'd changed her mind. *She'd changed her mind!* That I had left my company—which now refuses to take me back—was my problem, Tina said."

Jane looked at him. His face was dark red, his jaw muscles tight. His fists were clenched at his sides.

"If you're so angry at her, why did you have lunch with her and her husband today?"

"Why wouldn't I? She invited me. She's running Corsair—I can still sell books to her. I'm not an idiot."

Or are you, Jane wondered, *to have trusted Tina Vale?*

"What," she asked, "does any of this have to do with me?"

"Ah!" He smiled. "I've decided to go into partnership with someone else. I've thought about it long and hard, and the person I've decided to go into partnership with . . . is you."

She gaped at him. "But you don't even know me."

"I've been watching your career for some time. I've been impressed with your successes. That deal you made for Goddess, who I understand is as difficult a client as any agent could ever have, was nothing short of brilliant." In May of the previous year, Jane had sold the autobiography of Goddess, the pop star sensation, to Jack Layton when he was still at Corsair. The book, entitled *My Life on Top,* had been published the previous month and was still selling phenomenally well.

"Also," Mankewitz continued, "I knew your late husband, Kenneth. He and I had a number of projects together when he was an editor. I had enormous respect for him."

"Thank you."

"It would be an honor to work with you, as Mankewitz & Stuart."

Jane gazed up at him kindly, then gave her head a gentle shake. "I'm sorry. I'm extremely honored, truly, but I can't go into partnership with you."

"Why not?"

"I like my agency the way it is. I can come and go as I please, don't have to answer to anyone or be there for anyone. Besides, if I ever do take a partner, it would be Daniel, my assistant, who is becoming quite a good agent in his own right. It would be terribly unfair to overlook him."

"You have integrity, unlike Tina. I like that, respect it." He gave a courtly nod. "Very well. I'm sorry that that's your answer, but I respect it. What else can I say?" He took her hand in both of his and shook it warmly. "Thanks for hearing me out."

"Thank *you,*" she said, feeling sad for him, and watched as he turned, his hands in the pockets of his expensive black Italian suit, and headed along a path that ran around to the front of the hotel toward the parking lot.

Jane's cell phone rang as she reentered the hotel. It was Nick.

"Mom! Get over here! Winky's coming up soon."

"Okay, I'll be right there."

She hurried across the lobby to the cat show ballroom, remembering as she entered to be upbeat and enthusiastic. But Nick and Florence were anything but.

"Missus, may I speak with you for a moment?" Florence asked in her Trinidadian lilt.

The two women stepped away from the row of cages. "Is something the matter?" Jane asked.

"Yes," Florence said through gritted teeth, and tilted her head toward the woman at the cage to the left of Winky's. "She's a major piece of work. Gail, her name is."

"What's she been doing?"

"She's been making rude comments about Winky ever since we got here. *Her* cat, Tiger Lily, is perfect."

Jane peered at the woman. She was short and squat, with a mass of wavy purplish hennaed hair. She wore rumpled beige linen shorts with a matching top.

"*Her* cat," Florence went on, "is a shoo-in for the Household Pet finals. Winky, on the other hand, is 'mangy' and 'badly behaved.' "

"Mangy! Badly behaved!"

Jane walked over to the woman, who stood like a smiling soldier behind Tiger Lily's cage.

"You're Gail?" Jane said.

Gail turned to her, still smiling. "Do I know you?"

Jane pointed to Winky's cage. "That mangy, badly behaved cat belongs to me."

Gail's face grew stony. "What do you mean?"

"I hear you've been putting my cat down since she got here."

"Just trying to be helpful," Gail said sullenly.

"Keep it to yourself," Jane said, "or I'll stuff you into that cage with Tiger Lily. Got me?"

"Y-yes."

Jane ambled away, Nick and Florence's gazes fixed on her.

"She shouldn't be bothering you again."

"Thanks, Mom," Nick said, "but there's another problem."

"Another problem?"

"Look." Nick pointed to Winky's cage. Winky was rubbing herself wildly on the floor of the cage. Suddenly she rolled over, kicked her legs into the air three times, and started bouncing off the walls of the cage. "She's gone bananas!"

"Winky," Jane said, approaching the cage, "what's the matter with you?"

Florence said, "She's been doing this for the past half-hour, missus. Do you think all of this is making her nervous?"

"That must be it." Jane's voice was troubled. "Maybe we shouldn't have done this to her."

Gail approached them. "Don't worry, it'll be over soon for her. She won't make it to the finals."

Jane spun on her. "What did I just tell you? Keep your mouth shut, or I'll turn Tiger Lily into a collar for my winter coat."

Horrified, Gail shrunk back, eyes bulging.

"Now then," Jane resumed. "I think the best thing is to just leave her alone, let her calm down. The judging is soon, right? Let's just let it happen. You know how she takes to people. I'm sure she'll charm the pants off the judge."

"I don't know about that, Mom," Nick said worriedly. "The cat show rules say that cats in the Household Pet class"—he opened a brochure and read—"are judged for their uniqueness, pleasing appearance, unusual markings, and *sweet disposition.*"

"Winky has the sweetest disposition of any cat I know," Jane said.

"Yes, but you wouldn't know it from looking at her now!"

It was true. Winky was ping-ponging off the walls of her cage so fast she was practically a blur. Jane was reminded of the tiger in *Little Black Sambo*. Would Winky turn to butter?

"Definitely nervous," she said, her gaze fixed on the shaking cage.

"Missus!" Florence whispered.

The judge, a plump little man in a red polo shirt, had reached Tiger Lily's cage. He peered in, moving his head from side to side to study the cat from different angles. Finally he straightened, smiling, and hung a red-and-white ribbon on the cage.

"What's that?" Jane asked sourly.

"It's a merit ribbon," Florence explained. "Any cat that is healthy and well groomed gets one."

The judge moved on to Winky's cage and did a double take when he saw her on her back, kicking her paws into the air. "What's wrong with her?" he asked them.

"Excited to be here!" Jane burst out.

"Evidently," the judge replied dryly, and waited for Winky to slow down long enough to get a look at her. He hung a red-and-white merit ribbon on Winky's cage, but he was shaking his head sadly.

Gail was back. "Like I said, it doesn't look like she's going to make it to the finals."

Jane turned and gave her a dirty look. Then she

said to Nick and Florence, "I have to get back to the convention. Call me and let me know what happens."

"All right," Nick said dejectedly, and Jane planted a kiss on his soft brown hair before hurrying from the ballroom.

Jane had a busy afternoon. She sat on two romance panels, then took an hour's worth of one-on-one appointments with writers looking for agents. At three o'clock she had an appointment to have drinks with two of her clients, Elaine Lawler and Bertha Stumpf, who were friends. Jane spotted them outside the hotel's bar, a darkish fern-filled cave called Made in the Shade.

"Whoo-oo, Janey!" Bertha cried, wildly waving a pink handkerchief.

"Hello, ladies," Jane said. "Good to see you both."

Elaine gave Jane an air kiss. "Good to see you, too, Jane dear."

It never ceased to amaze Jane that two such very different people could be such close friends. Bertha, who wrote historical romances under the pseudonym Rhonda Redmond and whose royalty advances were quite high, was dumpy, in her late fifties, with coarse hair that was always some stark shade of yellow or orange. She wore too much jewelry, whined incessantly, and was, Jane decided, a classic narcissist.

Elaine, in contrast, was coolly elegant, tall and slim, with smartly cut brown hair, perfect makeup, and small discreet diamonds in her ears. She was gracious, never a bother, always grateful for anything Jane did for her. Her Regency romances earned very little for her and Jane, but that didn't matter to Jane. She just enjoyed working with Elaine.

"Let's get a table," Bertha said, suddenly fanning herself wildly with the handkerchief. "My feet are killing me."

They took a table at the back of the bar.

"I don't know why I ever agreed to do those one-on-ones," Bertha complained. "Those pathetic little women with their dreary ideas. I swear by the end of the hour they had all blended into one dreary woman!"

"Now, Bertha," Elaine said, "don't be unkind. After all, you and I were dreary women like that ourselves once."

"Speak for yourself," Bertha said. "Get the waitress."

Jane signaled to a young woman standing near the bar and she came over and took their drink order.

"Well," Jane said brightly, "how have you two been enjoying the convention? Aside from the dreary one-on-ones."

"The Fashion of Passion Pageant was a hoot," Elaine said. "Did I tell you that this year someone dressed up as one of my characters?"

"No," Jane said. "That's marvelous."

Bertha was gazing around the bar, not listening.

Elaine nodded. "I was thrilled. This sweet young woman who loves my books dressed up as Grace from my book *The Wicked Miss Wickham.*"

"I love it," Jane said. "What about you, Bertha? Did anyone dress up as one of your characters?"

"Hm? Oh—no. I'm glad, actually. None of those women could ever do my characters justice."

The waitress arrived with their drinks. Jane took a big sip of her Cosmopolitan. She always found Bertha easier to take after a drink or two.

"Oh, look," Bertha said, her gaze fixed on the lobby. "It's Dario!"

A tall, muscular man with a mane of black hair, wearing only a skimpy loincloth, strolled past the bar. Dario was currently the top male cover model. His famous face and body graced countless romance novels.

"Whoa!" Bertha cried. "Lemme at him."

"You and eight hundred other women," Elaine said with a laugh.

"I suppose you're right. He's probably dumb as dirt, anyway."

"Actually," Jane said, "I hear he's quite interesting. He's got a degree in botany or something."

"Mm," Bertha said, not listening. "Jane, I need to talk to you about something."

Jane turned to her.

"You know I've been very unhappy at Bantam. That girl they've got editing me," she said, referring to Harriet Green, "will never understand what I do. It's just not a good fit."

Not to mention that Bertha's sales had been declining for the past six books, Jane thought, but said nothing.

"Anyway," Bertha went on, "I heard some interesting gossip this morning that will help us."

"Bertha," Jane said uneasily, "I'd rather talk to you about this privately, okay?"

"Why?" Bertha squealed. "Elaine and I can say anything in front of each other, right, Elaine?"

Elaine nodded graciously.

"See? Well, the gossip I heard is that Salomé

Sutton is leaving Corsair. That leaves a lovely spot for *moi!*"

"How did you hear that?" asked Jane, who had no intention of telling the jealous and possessive Bertha that she would be working for Salomé.

"Actually, I heard it from Salomé herself."

"You spoke with her? I didn't even know you knew her?"

"No, I didn't speak with her, silly. I eavesdropped on a conversation she was having with someone else. She said that since some new woman has come to run Corsair—a Tina something—there was no place there for Salomé anymore."

"Really?" Elaine said. "Why not?"

"Because this Tina woman has brought Stephanie Queen from the publisher where she used to work. Salomé feels Stephanie will get all of the promotion dollars, and Salomé will be all but forgotten. So my plan is, Jane, for you to sell me to this Tina person. I'll take Salomé's place!"

"Bertha," Jane said, turning to her with a grimace, "that makes no sense at all. First of all, with all due respect, you are nowhere near Salomé Sutton's level. Second, if Corsair would ignore Salomé Sutton, why wouldn't they ignore you?"

"Because I am a better writer than Salomé Sutton," Bertha announced in perfect seriousness.

Jane gaped at her. "Have you ever read her?"

"No, but I've heard about her books. Trust me, Jane, I could really go places at a publisher like Corsair."

"No, you can't go places there, because Salomé isn't leaving—at least not yet. She's trying to buy back the last book of her current contract, but Corsair doesn't want to let her go."

Bertha stared at Jane in amazement. "How do you know all that?"

"Oh, eavesdropping, like you."

Bertha eyed her suspiciously.

"Jane," Elaine said, "let's talk about you. How have you been?"

"Me?" Jane put her hand to her heart. "A client is asking about me? Quick, my smelling salts!"

"Oh, stop it!" Elaine said, laughing. "You know I care how you are."

"That's right, you're the one." Jane gave Elaine a grateful smile, recalling that this was one more reason why she enjoyed working with this woman. "I'm fine, Elaine, thank you."

"Are you really? You're not . . . lonely?"

"Not at all. I have a boyfriend, you know."

"Ah! No, I didn't."

Bertha said, "Didn't I tell you? It's that cop."

Jane sighed. "He's a police detective. Right here in Shady Hills, in fact."

"What's his name?" Elaine asked.

"Stanley Greenberg."

Elaine's brows rose. "Jewish?" Elaine was Jewish.

Jane pondered this question. "Yes, I suppose he is, though he never talks about it. I'd say he's a nonpracticing Jew."

"Interesting," Elaine said.

"You don't miss Kenneth at all?" Bertha said, almost as if she hoped Jane did.

"Of course I do, Bertha. I always will. But as time goes on, the pain lessens. And as I said, I'm not lonely, because I have Stanley. He's a wonderful man."

At that moment, as if on cue, Stanley appeared at the entrance to the bar.

"There he is now!" Jane said, delighted. "Stanley!"

He came over to their table. "Ladies."

"Elaine Lawler, I'd like to introduce Stanley Greenberg."

Smiling, he shook Elaine's hand. "A pleasure."

"Bertha Stumpf—"

"Rhonda Redmond! You know I never use my real name in business venues. Besides," Bertha said, giving Stanley a sickly little smile, "we've met."

"Oh, that's right," Jane said. The previous December, at a writers' retreat in Shady Hills that Jane had organized and at which Bertha had been one of the instructors, there had been a murder, and Stanley had been among the officers investigating.

"Nice to see you again," Stanley said, "under more pleasant circumstances."

Bertha didn't reply, and Stanley shifted his gaze awkwardly to Jane. "Well, I'd better get back to work. Nice to see you, ladies."

They watched him walk away.

"He's adorable," Elaine said. "Love that hair over his forehead. Like a little boy."

"He's a good man," Jane said.

"What's he doing here?" Bertha asked.

"Making sure there's no trouble. There's a cat show going on, and the hotel overbooked. The cat people are fighting with the RAT people. Stanley's making sure everyone behaves."

"I suppose he hasn't got any more pressing matters to attend to," Bertha said dryly, and rose. "Jane, since you don't seem to think my idea of moving to Corsair is a good one, I guess we don't have anything more to talk about."

Elaine looked shocked.

"Bertha," Jane said, "we're here to have a friendly drink, remember?"

Bertha looked down at her empty glass. "We have! Later, ladies." And she waddled away.

"I'm sorry, Jane," Elaine said, looking embarrassed.

"What have you got to be sorry for?" Jane asked.

"I don't know. I guess I always feel I have to apologize for Bertha."

"Frankly, I don't understand why you two are friends at all."

Elaine shrugged uncomfortably. "She was kind to me when I was just getting started. Now . . . I feel sorry for her. She really has no friends."

"You're a good soul, Elaine Lawler," Jane said, and patted the other woman affectionately on the shoulder.

Jane's cell phone began to ring. "Excuse me," she said, and answered it. It was Nick.

"The show's over, Mom."

"Over?"

"For us, anyway." He sounded dejected. "That woman Gail was right—Winky didn't make the finals. So we're going home. We'll see you later."

Putting away her phone, Jane noticed groups of women passing the bar, obviously on their way to some event.

"Are you going?" Elaine asked.

"To what?"

"The award ceremony. That Tina person Bertha was talking about is getting a Lifetime Achievement Award from RAT. Come on, we'll sit together."

Jane couldn't think of anything she would enjoy

less than attending the award ceremony for Tina, but at that moment she couldn't think of a gracious way to bow out. "All right."

Together they made their way to a large function room at the far end of the lobby. The room was already nearly full of women, all buzzing excitedly. Jane and Elaine took seats near the back.

At the front of the room, Kara Falcone, RAT's charismatic president, stood behind a podium, gazing out at the audience. Kara, a tall, big-boned blonde with prominent teeth, tapped gently on the microphone and burst into a horsy smile. "Good afternoon, ladies and gentlemen." The audience grew quiet. "I'm sure you're all as excited as I am about this event. We're here to present a Romance Authors Together Lifetime Achievement Award to a very special person . . . someone I'd like to tell you about now."

Kara cleared her throat. "Tina Vale, our honoree today, was a top literary agent before deciding to become an editor—a decision for which we as romance readers are extremely grateful."

The audience broke into spirited applause.

Jane turned to Elaine. "I think I'm going to be sick."

Kara continued, "In her new role as editor, Tina Vale immediately began to make her mark on the world of women's fiction. She made a point of making sure there were always plenty of romances and women's mainstream novels on her publication lists. In doing so, she discovered some of the legends of romance. It's a long list, but I want to read it to you now, so that you can get the full impact of the achievements of this remarkable woman."

A wave of nausea rose in Jane's throat. She

couldn't take any more. She turned to Elaine. "I'm really sorry," she whispered, "but I've got to go."

Elaine looked concerned. "Are you all right?"

"Oh sure, I'm fine. Gotta call home, make sure my son is all right." And she jumped up and scooted out the door.

Outside in the lobby, it was mercifully tranquil, since everyone at the convention was in that room listening to the long list of Tina Vale's discoveries. Breathing in the lovely cool air, Jane caught the aroma of food cooking—steak, it smelled like. She realized she was hungry. The convention dinner banquet would immediately follow Tina's award ceremony, which with any luck would be over soon. Jane made a mental note not to sit with Bertha.

She delved into a new area of the lobby's jungle, following a brick path around a cage containing two cockatiels. She came out into a small tree-sheltered circle of brick on which sat a comfortable-looking loveseat and a coffee table.

"Perfect," she breathed, and settled into the loveseat. Looking about her, she was pleased to discover that she was completely hidden from the lobby itself.

Opening her purse, she took out her compact, checked her makeup, and put on some more lipstick. She gazed over at the cockatiels, sitting silently on their perch. From the room in which the award ceremony was taking place came Kara Falcone's voice, as if very far away. ". . . and I can think of no one more deserving of the Romance Authors Together Lifetime Achievement Award. Ladies and gentlemen, I am honored to present to you a titan of the romance world, and a fine human being . . ."

Obviously Kara didn't know her.

". . . Tina Vale!"

Wild applause, which seemed to go on forever before finally dying down. Jane waited for the sound of Tina's voice thanking everyone. Instead, there was an odd silence. Then came a murmur of many puzzled voices. Jane frowned. What had happened?

She heard heels clicking on the tile of the lobby just behind her, and turning on the loveseat, parted two palm fronds to peer out. Two convention coordinators had emerged from the award room, concerned expressions on their faces.

"Where do you think she is?" one asked the other, who shrugged.

"Do you think she forgot?"

"Forgot! A Lifetime Achievement Award? No way. Something must be wrong."

A third woman appeared. "Is she here?" The other two shook their heads. "I'll go up to her suite to see if there's a problem." She hurried off to the elevators.

Jane settled back into the loveseat. Wasn't that just like Tina to blow off her award. It wasn't at all surprising, really, considering what she had just done to Nat Barre . . . and Jory Mankewitz . . . and Salomé Sutton. That list went on and on, too.

Behind her she heard more clacking of heels on tile, as the murmur of voices in the award room grew louder. She turned again and peeked out. The coordinator who had gone up to Tina's suite had reappeared and was speaking to the other two women. "I knocked on her door. No answer."

"Did you knock loud?"

"Of course I knocked loud. She's not in there, or if she is, she's sound asleep."

"What if she's sick or something?"

The third woman looked at her, clearly considering this possibility seriously. "You know, she could be. Like I said, no one would ever just forget she was getting this award. I know what to do." She marched over to the reception desk, where Andrew Cowan, the hotel manager, busied himself behind two clerks. The woman got his attention and spoke to him. He listened, an intense expression on his face, then came out from behind the counter and followed her to the elevators. They both went up together.

Jane sat back down and rolled her eyes. She giggled. Wait until the RATs found out Tina simply hadn't bothered to come down and claim her award! She was probably doing her nails, or balancing her checkbook.

Approximately ten minutes passed before Jane heard the elevator doors swoosh open. She turned and resumed her spying. The woman walked slowly out of the elevator, a sickly expression on her face, which had gone very pale. Immediately behind her was Andrew Cowan, who was chewing on two fingernails at the same time.

"Call an ambulance!" the woman suddenly shrieked at him.

"No, the police," Cowan said, and ran for the front desk.

An ambulance? The police? Had Tina been hurt?

Stanley was probably still in the hotel. Jane

called him on her cell phone and he answered instantly.

"Where are you?" she asked.

"Back in Conference Room D. They're still fighting. I may have to have one of them arrested," he joked.

"Stanley, the hotel manager is calling the police."

"Why?"

"Something about Tina Vale." She made her way out of the sheltered circle, back along the brick path, and into the lobby proper. At the far end, Stanley emerged from Conference Room D. She waved to him and he waved back, closing his phone and hurrying to the reception desk. There he spoke with Cowan for a moment before hurrying after him to the elevators.

Jane stood, waiting. It felt like an eternity. Finally she could stand it no longer and called Stanley again.

"Jane," he said, his voice grave, "I can't talk to you now. Tina's dead."

Chapter Six

Jane fell back against the lobby wall. Tina, *dead*?
Word spread quickly. People poured from the award room, chattering animatedly among themselves. Scared-looking coordinators ran back and forth, as if trying to herd the convention attendees but without knowing exactly where.

"Ladies and gentlemen!" came Kara Falcone's shrill voice, and the crowd grew quiet, turning to her. She stood a little above them on a low set of steps into the lobby gardens. "We've had some bad news. Please, we're now going directly into dinner in the grand ballroom. Down this corridor," she said, pointing, and the mass began to move.

As eager as Jane was for information about Tina, she no longer wanted to attend the banquet; she wanted to go home. She'd speak to Stanley later anyway, get the full scoop. Before anyone could spot her, she hurried out the hotel's entrance to her car and got onto Route 46.

She got off on Packer Road. On the left was the house whose top floor was Daniel and Ginny's apartment. Wait until Daniel heard about Tina, she thought. Then she passed the fire station before turning right into the hills on Oakmont Avenue. The last tarnished light of this summer day gave Shady Hills an enchanted quality—a feeling of unbreakable tranquility. How deceiving that feeling could be, Jane had discovered too many times.

She turned left onto her own street, Lilac Way, and climbed the hill to her house, a brown chalet-style Tudor on the left, behind a high holly hedge. Pulling into the driveway, she saw Nick and Florence tossing a Frisbee at the side of the house. The white flying saucer sailed high over Nick's head and he ran toward Jane, laughing.

"Mom! You weren't supposed to be back till tonight."

"I know." She gave him a chipper smile. "Change of plans."

Florence was eyeing her suspiciously. "Missus . . . what happened?"

Jane laughed. "I can't put one over on you two, can I? Well, if you must know, Tina Vale, who was supposed to receive a Lifetime Achievement Award this afternoon, died."

Florence put a hand to her mouth. "Died?"

"Mm. I don't know the details yet. Stanley will tell me."

Jane entered the house through the garage. Florence was already in the kitchen, waiting for her. "Are you okay, missus?"

"Me? I'm fine. Tired, that's all."

"Aren't you even curious about how Tina Vale died?"

"Yes, of course I am. But we all know it must have been some kind of unfortunate accident. We just don't know the details yet."

"Have you had any dinner?"

"No. Haven't eaten much at all today, actually."

"Then you will have some of my shrimp salad." Florence took a large plastic-covered bowl from the refrigerator.

"Florence, you are a marvel." Jane peeked into the bowl. "Mm, that looks heavenly."

"A special Trinidad recipe my mother just e-mailed me. Even Master Nicholas liked it. For him I left out the rum."

"Rum? In a salad?" Jane winked at her. "You'll have to make it just for us some time."

"You got it, missus. Now sit and I will have it on the table in a flash."

Jane obeyed. Suddenly she felt washed out, as if her bones had turned to jelly. Florence placed a plate of shrimp salad in front of her and she began to eat. "This is marvelous."

"Thank you. Perfect for a hot summer day." Florence sat down opposite Jane. "So this Tina who died—she is the one who has been giving you so much trouble, yes?"

"That's right."

"Your Mr. Barre should be pleased at this news."

Jane looked up at her. "What do you mean?"

Florence shrugged. "Just that maybe now his book will be published after all. Wasn't she the one who didn't like it?"

"Yes," Jane said thoughtfully. "You're absolutely right. Yes, this may put a whole new light on things."

* * *

Stanley stopped by a couple of hours later, his bearing grim. Jane took him into her study off the living room and they sat in armchairs in the corner of the room with glasses of iced tea. Winky appeared and with an angry-sounding yowl jumped into Jane's lap, circled endlessly, and finally curled into a fur ball. "You're mad at us for subjecting you to that nasty cat show, aren't you, Wink?" Jane said.

In the next instant, Twinky, the only kitten that Jane had kept of the litter to which Winky had given birth the previous Christmas, jumped onto Stanley's lap. Twinky was an exact duplicate of Winky, but in miniature. She, too, curled into a ball and went to sleep.

With his big rough hand Stanley softly petted the sleeping kitten, his thoughts clearly elsewhere.

"So?" Jane said. "What happened?"

"What do you mean?"

She rolled her eyes. "What happened to Tina? How did she die?"

He drew in his breath, cleared his throat. "Jane, you know I don't like to discuss police business with you."

"Oh, Stanley, please don't start that again. You know you're going to wind up telling me everything, so let's just get it over with."

He thought about this, then nodded as if to say Jane made good sense. "All right. She killed herself."

"Killed herself! Tina Vale? I don't believe it."

"Believe what you like, but it's true."

"Nope. Never. Tina Vale would never commit suicide. She loved herself too much to do that."

He gazed at her through narrowed eyes. "Mm. It's true, though. There was a note."

"Really? What did it say?"

"That she couldn't go on."

"And how did she 'kill herself'?"

"Dropped a plugged-in toaster into her bath. Electrocuted."

"Toasted," she said, and couldn't suppress a giggle.

"Jane, that's in very bad taste."

"Yes, you're right, I'm sorry. How awful. I think I saw the toaster in question."

"Oh?"

"When I was in Tina's suite, her husband came in with one he'd found at a local antique shop."

"Sounds like the one. It was definitely old. Strange-looking thing." He gazed absently down at the sleeping kitten, stroked its slowly rising and falling tummy.

She was watching him. "What?"

He looked up. "Hm?"

"What are you thinking?"

"Nothing."

Gently she took his chin in her hand and turned his head to face her. "Tell me."

He laughed. "You know me too well. First of all, if this woman collected toasters, you'd think she would have known enough to keep them away from the water."

She nodded. "Go on."

"Second, from everything you've told me about Tina during this Nat Barre situation, she just wasn't the suicide type. She had everything going for her—a new, high-level job at Corsair, a handsome, adoring husband . . ."

"Stop. Not sure about that."

"What do you mean?"

"When he came in this morning, he kissed her on the forehead as if she were his sister. And as for her adoring him, I don't think so. She told us flat out that she was having an affair with Rafe Parker, Corsair's chairman. *And* that the only man she ever really loved was my Kenneth."

Stanley looked down uneasily, as if not wanting her to talk about something he knew hurt her so much. Then he looked up again. "There's another reason. Something Ian noticed."

"Yes?"

"He said there were three keys to the suite. Shelly Adams, the secretary, had one, but she threw it at Tina when she quit her job and stormed out. Ian was standing there when it happened.

"Tina had a key. We found it on her dresser in the bedroom.

"Ian had the third key. Whenever he was in the suite, he kept it in an ashtray on a table near the door. When he left for his toaster-seeking expedition this morning, he forgot to take the key, leaving it in the ashtray. He remembered dropping it there. Now it's gone. Which means that someone who was in the suite between the time Ian left and now, took it."

She looked at him, her eyes wide. "And used it later to get into the suite, kill Tina, and leave a fake suicide note?"

"Right. Which, by the way, Ian has examined. It's definitely his wife's handwriting. We're going to compare it to other samples, just to be sure." He looked away uneasily.

"I know what you're thinking," she said. "*I* was

one of the people in the suite this morning. Are you saying I'm a murderer?"

"No, of course not. I know you better than that. But not everyone does, Jane. And you did have a very good motive."

It was true. Tina hadn't yet told Corsair's legal department to terminate Nat's contract. Now, as Florence had already pointed out, the novel's publication was virtually assured.

"*But,*" she said quickly, "there were other people in that suite today, and now that I think about it, they all had excellent motives, too."

Briefly she told him the stories that Shelly Adams, Salomé Sutton, and Jory Mankewitz had told her. "They all hated Tina for what she'd done to them."

"True," he admitted. "And of course others in the suite—at least, who are known about—were Ian Stein, who has no motive that we know of yet, and Nathaniel Barre, who had an excellent motive: $900,000, less your commission."

He checked his watch. "Ooh, I've gotta run. I told Linda and Ashley I'd be there for dinner," he said, referring to his divorced sister and her thirteen-year-old daughter, who lived at the north end of Shady Hills. "I'll see you soon."

She saw him to the door, where they kissed. She watched him get into his car and drive up Lilac Way. Closing the door, she was suddenly aware of Florence standing behind her in the foyer.

"What happened, missus? How did Tina Vale die?"

"Not sure. Maybe suicide, maybe not."

"But *how* did she die?"

"Toaster fell in the bathtub, electrocuted her."

"How awful." Florence frowned. "She was making toast in the bathtub?"

Jane had to laugh. "No, Florence, she collected antique toasters."

"Ah! I saw a Martha Stewart program about that. But if she collected them, wouldn't she have known not to use one near water?"

"You'd think so."

"What are you saying, missus?"

Jane turned to face Florence. "Stanley thinks it may not have been suicide. There was a note, supposedly in Tina's handwriting, but it could have been faked. She said she couldn't go on. Why not? Everything was going well in her life."

"Then—"

"Stanley thinks it could have been murder. Because a key went missing. Someone in the suite between early this morning and the time Tina died grabbed that key and used it later to slip back in and kill her."

"Someone in the suite? But, missus, there must have been a number of people in the suite, no?"

"Yes, there were," Jane said. "And one of them was me."

Florence stared at her for a moment; then understanding came into her eyes and her jaw dropped. "Oh, missus!"

Chapter Seven

Jane slept badly. She dreamed she was standing at the edge of a massive black bathtub in which Tina Vale soaked among heaping clouds of soap-suds. In Jane's hands was a toaster. "The toast walks through the slot in the center," she told Tina.

"Give it to me," Tina said, reaching for it.

Jane held it out as if to hand it to her, then suddenly opened her hands. The toaster hit the water and there was a terrible hissing sound. Simultaneously, Tina began to melt into the water, which had turned dark red from her blood.

She awoke with a start. The clock on her night table said 4:17. She closed her eyes, tried to get back to sleep, yet she never really slept until the alarm went off at 6:30. She got up, washed her face, brushed her teeth, then remembered it was Sunday. She was going back to the convention today, but hadn't planned on being there before ten. With a groan she climbed back into bed and closed her eyes, but it was no use. She showered, put on her robe, and in the quiet, sun-filled kitchen fed Winky and Twinky and made herself a cup of strong coffee.

She saw all the ramifications of the situation now. She was a murder suspect. And she would have to clear her name—fast—before word got out and ruined her career.

She could see it now: attending a meeting of the Association of Authors' Representatives, catching people throwing her wondering glances. Having lunch with an editor, this question looming huge between them.

She knew she hadn't killed Tina Vale. The only way to clear her good name and save her reputation, her livelihood, was to find out who had.

She would have to do some investigating on her own.

With a sinking feeling she trudged back upstairs and dressed for the convention in a pale green pant suit. Florence and Nick were still asleep when she left the house.

She arrived at the Windmere a little after ten. She was scheduled to appear on a panel at 10:30. Walking into the lobby, she stopped short. Standing on the edge of a fountain was Dario, the cover model, wearing a different, dark-brown loincloth. He stood, arms at his sides, chin up, as if posing for a cover shoot. Then Jane realized that he was, in fact, posing for a photographer standing just to Jane's left.

"Don't get any ideas," a deep male voice whispered in her ear. She spun around.

"Stanley! What are you doing here? Working on—" She tilted her head upward, toward Tina's suite, and lifted a brow questioningly.

"No, not for the moment. The Chief asked me to come back to make sure everything goes smoothly, especially in light of—" He copied Jane's head tilt. "I also have to make sure there's no more bickering about that room. Would you believe those women were still arguing about it *last night?*"

"Oh, I believe it."

The photographer flashed away. "Lift your hand to your eyes as if you're searching for someone," he called to Dario, who immediately obliged.

Stanley's shoulders rose in a laugh. "The Hunk-a-Thon is today, did you know that?"

Jane nodded boredly. She was quite familiar with this event, in which hopeful male models competed for the title of Mr. Romance. Many past winners of this contest had gone on to successful cover modeling careers.

Finally the photographer was finished, and Dario stepped down from the fountain and walked directly over to Jane and Stanley. "Excuse me," he said to Stanley with a thick Italian accent. "Are you a policeman?"

Stanley drew back in surprise. "Yes."

"Ah, *eccellentissimo!* The hotel manager, he pointed you out to me and said I should speak to you."

"About what?"

"About what happened to Miss Vale. A terrible tragedy."

That wasn't the word Jane would have used, but she kept this thought to herself.

"Yes . . ." Stanley began.

"She was my dear friend. A marvelous woman. Very kind. I cannot believe she is gone. How could she have done such a horrid thing to herself?"

Clearly embarrassed, Stanley shook his head. "I really can't discuss it."

But I can, Jane thought. "You go on, Stanley. I'll catch up with you later."

He gave her an odd look, then nodded and walked off toward the reception desk.

"My name is Jane Stuart," she said to Dario, then lowered her voice. "I'm a literary agent. I've got to do a panel in a few minutes, but if you're free at eleven-thirty, I'd like to talk to you."

He looked puzzled. "About what?"

"About Tina. I knew her quite well."

"Ah," he breathed. "Very good. Eleven-thirty. Where shall I meet you?"

"I'll come to your room."

He drew back slightly, giving her a surprised look.

"Just to talk," she said. "What's your room number?"

"Penthouse A."

She blinked in surprise. "Right, got it. See you then."

Stepping off the elevator, she looked to the left and saw that the door to Penthouse B, Tina's suite, had been crisscrossed with bright yellow barrier tape: POLICE LINE DO NOT CROSS.

Dario opened the door to Penthouse A wearing a red-and-gold paisley silk robe. He looked past her at the taped door and grimaced. "I have to get out of here. I asked the hotel to give me a new suite, but they say no, there are no others available."

"Full up."

"Scusa?"

"Nothing. Sorry."

"Please," he said, closing the door behind her, "tell me your name again."

"Jane. Jane Stuart."

"May I call you Jane?"

"Of course," she said, taking a seat in the living room.

"Coffee?"

"Love some."

He brought mugs of coffee for both of them and sat down opposite her. "Now, how did you know Tina?"

"As I said, I'm a literary agent. She and I have . . . worked together."

"I see! So a literary agent—that is what?"

Jane hated explaining what she did. But she gave him a pleasant smile. "I represent writers, sell their books for them." Surely he could understand that.

He frowned. "You sell their books for them? Forgive my ignorance, but can they not sell their own books?"

"Certainly—if they want to, and if the publisher they want to sell to will read unagented material. Let me put it another way. I'm like the writer's manager."

"Ah, *sì!* A manager. I have a manager. A very good man who gets me jobs. Same thing." He smiled modestly. "A very good job my manager has gotten me, in Hollywood."

"Really?"

He nodded quickly, like a little boy. "I will be the Spray-Away Man!"

She wrinkled her brow. "The Spray-Away Man?"

"*Sì*. Spray-Away, it is a product you buy in the grocery market. You spray it in your pan instead of butter."

"Oh, yes, of course. And you'll be promoting this product?"

"In a commercial, *sì*. I will magically appear in a woman's kitchen—*poof!* in a puff of smoke—just as she is about to put butter in her frying pan to make the eggs. I will say, 'Stop! Got weight you want to lose today? Don't use butter—spray away!' Then we cut to the woman eating the eggs, and she says, 'I can't believe this isn't butter.' And I smile and say 'Spray-Away! Instead of butter, every day!' "

"My my," she said politely, "that is impressive. Congratulations."

He gave a gracious nod and laughed. "Now that we know what we do, let us talk about poor Tina."

"Yes. I'm terribly sorry for your loss. You said you and she were close friends."

He looked at her earnestly. "I loved her very much. She was everything to me, yet there is no one I can tell—except you. For no one knew of our love."

"Then you were more than just friends."

"I have no shame," he said, a little defensively, "that Tina was a married woman. She said she did not love him." He leaned forward. "Please, is there nothing you can tell me about how she died? You seemed to be a friend of the policeman."

She shook her head helplessly. "I'm sorry, I know only what you know—that she killed herself. Though I find that highly unlike Tina."

"As do I! It makes no sense. I do not believe it."

"Tell me, Dario, do you know of anyone who might have wanted to kill her?"

His dark brown eyes grew huge. "Kill! But she was not killed. She committed suicide."

She knew she couldn't go so far as to tell him about the keys, so she just shrugged while giving one eyebrow a meaningful lift.

"You think Tina was murdered? No! This I cannot believe." He thought for a moment. "But wait! Maybe I can believe it. The other night, when Tina was in my arms, I asked her if something was bothering her. She didn't seem herself. She told me that someone—I think it was an agent, like you!—but a man, a Mank-something, was furious at her."

"Go on."

"He had threatened to kill her. When I asked Tina what she could have done to make this man so angry at her, she said she had changed her mind about a business deal. Tell me," he demanded, "how could a man be angry enough about a business matter to want to kill over it?"

"Did you ask Tina that?"

"I did, but she didn't answer me."

"I see. Is there anything else that comes to mind? Anything else Tina might have mentioned about someone being angry at her?"

"No, nothing that I can recall." He leaned forward again, catching his lower lip between his perfect white teeth. "Jane, you won't tell anyone about Tina and me, will you?"

"No, of course not. That's between us."

He breathed a sigh of relief. "Thank you. Because I would not want the police thinking that I would have had any reason to hurt Tina. In truth, she and I had spoken of a project together—something that will now not happen—so aside from my loving her so, I needed her for this."

"A project? What kind of project?"

"A book. A book about me. We were going to call it simply *Dario*. It was going to be a big tea table book, how you call it . . . ?"

"A coffee-table book."

"Thank you, a coffee-table book. It was to be a collection of my most famous romance novel covers, and next to them photographs of me in related poses." He blushed. "For all my lady fans, you know."

"Absolutely. What a great idea."

"Indeed!" he said, becoming animated. "And I was going to get a big advance for this book, maybe one hundred thousand dollars! My manager said he would be able to sell rights to a publisher in Italy, and also sell merchandising rights."

Jane studied him shrewdly. "For someone who didn't know what an agent was, you seem to know a lot about publishing."

For a brief moment he stared at her, as if sizing her up. "It is 'agent' I never heard of. I have a manager who does this work for me. That is all."

"Of course," she said, rising. "Thank you for the coffee. And my condolences on your loss."

"Thank you," he said, walking her to the door.

Suddenly he **check**ed his watch. "Oh my goodness!
I must run. I **am** the star of the Hunk-a-Thon in
twenty minutes **and** I have not oiled my body."

"Oh, dear. Well, I'll let you get to it, then."

He shut the door quickly behind her. Deep in
thought, Jane walked to the elevator and pressed
the DOWN button.

Stepping off the elevator, Jane saw Nat Barre
walking across the lobby toward the reception
desk. "Nat!"

She hurried up to him. "What are you doing
here? I thought for sure you'd be gone by last
night."

"I decided to stay for the whole convention. I
booked a room here in the hotel last night." He
shuffled uncomfortably. "I suppose you've heard
about Tina."

"Yes."

"I was no fan of hers, obviously, but I certainly
never wished her dead."

"Of course not. Well," she said, changing the
subject, "have you had a good time?"

"Heck, yes—a great time. A whole new world has
opened up to me."

Then Jane saw why. Shelly Adams, in a neat
plum-colored skirt and pink blouse, suddenly appeared and took Nat's arm. Nat beamed, blushing.
"I'll probably be staying in the area for a while.
Now if you'll excuse us . . ."

"Of course." She watched them join a stream of
people heading for Conference Room D, the
room the RATs and the cats had been fighting

over. Beside the door was a handwritten sign that said "Hunk-a-Thon."

Jane entered the room and took a seat at the back.

"Couldn't stay away, eh?"

She looked up. Bertha stood a few feet away, wiggling her eyebrows. She nestled her large bottom into the seat next to Jane's and giggled. "I have to confess this is my favorite part of the convention. All these gorgeous men give me ideas for my books."

Kara Falcone's voice boomed from the dais that had been set up at the front of the room. "Ladies and gentlemen, welcome to the Romance Authors Together Hunk-a-Thon. Have you all got your ballots?"

Jane looked around and saw that all the women around her held long white cards.

"Where's yours?" Bertha asked.

"That's okay, I don't think I'll be staying for the whole show."

Bertha shrugged. "Your loss." She gazed forward hungrily.

Kara went on, "The host of our show tonight is a very special man. You've seen his face and body on the covers of some of the most successful romances. Soon you'll see him on television as the Spray-Away Man! Ladies and gentlemen—Dario!"

The audience broke into wild applause and raucous whistles. Dario strode onto the stage, now wearing a tiger-print Tarzan number. His body glistened with oil.

"Oh, yumma," Bertha breathed. "Isn't he heaven?"

Jane, who would take Stanley over Dario any day, politely nodded.

Dario said a few words, then began introducing the contestants—men dressed as knights, wrestlers, and Vikings, men in G-strings, karate pants, and bikinis. Soon they all began to look alike to Jane. "I've got to go," she whispered to Bertha.

Bertha stared at her. "You're kidding."

"No. May I get out, please?"

"Suit yourself." Bertha got up and Jane squeezed past her.

"See you later," Jane whispered, and hurried out to the lobby. Suddenly she felt extremely tired, no doubt because she'd slept so badly the night before. Another cup of coffee would do her good, she decided, and headed for Tuscany Hills.

The restaurant was empty except for a man sitting way in the back. As Jane was seated, she noticed the man getting up and walking toward her. Looking up, she realized it was Jory Mankewitz.

"Oh, hello," she said pleasantly.

"Mind if I join you?"

What else did they have to talk about? She considered asking politely if he'd mind if she had some private time, but then Dario's words rang in her ears and she said, "That would be lovely."

He sat down opposite her. "Not at the Hunk-a-Thon, I see."

"I tried, but once you've seen one musclebound god, you've seen them all."

"True," he said with a laugh. A waiter came and they both ordered coffee. Mankewitz looked up at her, his expression serious. "Given any further thought to our conversation yesterday?"

"To be honest, no. I'm extremely flattered, really. But that kind of arrangement is not for me. I'm afraid the answer really is no."

He put up his hands as if to signify he wouldn't bring it up again. "Fair enough. But we can still be friends, right? I like you, Jane Stuart."

She gave him a gracious smile. "Why, thank you, Mr. Mankewitz. I like you, too."

"Please, call me Jory."

"Jory."

He fingered his napkin, wrapped it around his index finger. "A lot has happened since our last conversation."

"Yes, it has."

"Quite a shocker. Tina never struck me as the suicidal type."

"Me, neither," Jane said, watching him closely. "But what else could have happened?"

His expression grew dark. "Don't play games with me, Jane. You know what the police think happened."

"Do I? What's that?"

"That she was murdered."

"And how do you know that?"

"I know people who know people on the police force in this burg." His gaze met hers frankly. "I see now that my display of anger with you yesterday was badly timed."

She waved it away. "Don't give it another thought. I don't blame you for being angry."

He smiled. "Good. Thank you."

"Although," she said, "I have heard that you were *so* angry at Tina that you threatened to kill her."

"Who told you that?"

"People who know people."

"Fair enough. Actually, I did say that to Tina, but they were only words—my anger talking. After all, how would *you* feel if that had been done to you? I'm in big trouble now, do you see that?"

"No, frankly I don't."

"As I told you, Paul Donnelly, my former partner, won't take me back. I can't blame him. So that's out. And I'm not going to take a step down by working for one of the other large literary agencies in New York. Mankewitz & Donnelly was the most successful agency of them all.

"No, the only way to go forward is to go on my own, but I won't have the clout I had when I was partners with Paul. Or that I would have had as Mankewitz & Vale. Or Mankewitz & Stuart."

She gave him a reprimanding look.

"Sorry, sorry. You're right—I said I wouldn't bring it up again. But you see what I'm saying. Because of what Tina did to me, my career is badly damaged."

He gulped down the rest of his coffee and placed the cup in the saucer with a clatter. "But it's academic, isn't it—how angry I was at Tina, whether I could really have killed her—because in truth she committed suicide. She'd left a note. It's definitely her handwriting."

"But why would she have killed herself? Why wouldn't she have been able to 'go on'? It doesn't make sense."

He shrugged. "In many cases of suicide, no one ever suspected the torment going on in the victim's head."

"Maybe," she conceded. "I just can't see it in this instance."

He rose, shook his head. "And maybe no one

ever will. But the fact remains that something was making Tina Vale so unhappy that she couldn't go on living. Now, you'll excuse me? I have a client to meet."

"Of course. Thanks for joining me."

He took her hand, brought it to his lips, and gently kissed it. Then he walked slowly out of the restaurant. She watched him go, slim and sleek in his black Italian suit.

Chapter Eight

Jane nearly forgot she was scheduled to appear on another panel at three o'clock. Entering the room where her panel was supposed to take place, she was surprised to discover that her fellow panelists were Salomé Sutton and Stephanie Queen, whom Jane had never met. She was a plump woman who appeared to be in her late fifties, with an attractive round face surrounded by pretty brown hair in a feathery cut.

The panel's moderator, a convention coordinator who introduced herself as Marla Simms, introduced Jane to Stephanie, who looked up for a moment, said a quick "Hi," and returned her attention to the task of standing up a copy of her latest novel on the table before her. Salomé, seeing this, bent over, fished a copy of her latest romance out of her bag, and propped it up in front of her.

Marla announced that the subject of the panel was "Where Is Romance Going?" and asked Jane to say a few words first, from the agent's perspective.

Jane, who had given variations on this theme countless times, spoke of the trend toward contemporary romances, and the huge upsurge of romantic
suspense.

At this, Stephanie Queen beamed and patted
the top of her book. A number of people in the audience laughed.

A woman at the back of the room raised her
hand. "Where do you think romance—particularly
yours, Miss Queen—is going now that Tina Vale is
dead?"

Marla looked scandalized. "I think that's hardly
an appropriate question—"

"No, no, that's okay," Stephanie said. "It's a fair
question. Tina brought me to Corsair Publishing
from Bleecker Books. She had big plans for me.
But keep in mind that big plans are not made by
one person alone. Tina had the support of the
whole terrific Corsair team, and though we will
miss Tina terribly, that team is still in place."

Jane glanced at Salomé, who was rolling her
eyes.

Another woman in the audience asked, "What
about you, Miss Sutton? You're a Corsair veteran.
Will Tina's death affect your career in any way, do
you think?"

Jane watched her, wondering what she would
say.

"Stephanie is right," Salomé answered at last.
"That team she's referring to has been making my
books *New York Times* bestsellers for years. I, too,
will miss Tina, but the people who have con-
tributed so importantly to my success are all still
there."

A horse-faced woman in a tan jumpsuit raised

her hand. "They say Tina Vale was the meanest woman in publishing. There's also a rumor that she was murdered." A loud murmur rose from the crowd. "Any idea who might have knocked her off?"

Marla jumped to her feet. "Excuse me, but I can't allow that question to stand. Please, if you can't stick to the topic at hand, leave the room."

"I'd like to answer that question," Stephanie said, and the room grew quiet. She took a deep breath and looked deeply thoughtful for a moment, as if deciding on the best way to put her feelings into words. "This business of publishing is one of the most gossipy businesses of them all, and a lot of people have fun tearing other people apart. For some reason, the sport of maligning Tina Vale—calling her the meanest woman in publishing, saying she was a monster—has become quite popular.

"I worked with Tina for five years, and I can tell you that she was the kindest, most supportive, most thoughtful editor—and friend—a writer could ever have. Was she tough? Sure. Hard? Absolutely, when she needed to be. But as you've heard before, when a man is these things, we say he's a shark and admire him. When it's a woman we're talking about, we say she's a bitch or a barracuda."

Stephanie looked directly at the woman in the tan jumpsuit. "I would appreciate it if we could honor the memory of this remarkable woman by refraining from that kind of drooling gossip. I think it's the least she deserves."

At the words "drooling gossip" the horse-faced woman's jaw had dropped. Affronted, she jumped up from her chair and stormed out of the room. Spontaneously the audience broke into enthusiastic applause. Stephanie Queen gazed down at the table solemnly.

Drama queen, Jane thought with an inward roll of her eyes. These women were such a bunch of hypocrites. Then she noticed Salomé applauding and nodding in agreement, and thought she was going to be sick.

Mercifully, the panel ended ten minutes later. Out in the lobby, surrounded by the women who had attended the panel, hearing them buzz about what Stephanie Queen had said, Jane realized she couldn't get out of the hotel fast enough. She had no further events scheduled. She headed purposefully for the door.

"Jane!"

She spun around. Salomé Sutton bustled toward her with surprising speed. When she reached Jane she was huffing and puffing, perspiration on her upper lip. "Could you believe that bullshit Stephanie Queen was giving us about that bitch?"

Jane smirked. "I saw you applauding."

"What was I supposed to do? It was the polite thing. The political thing." Salomé's lip curled. "She's so full of it. She hated Tina."

"Really? Why?"

"Because Tina made her all kinds of promises to get her to leave Bleecker Books and go to Corsair with her. Now it appears none of those promises are going to be kept."

"Well," Jane said, "let's be fair. Tina is gone . . ."

"No, they weren't going to be kept even when Tina was alive!"

"How do you know this?"

"Stephanie and I have a friend in common. My friend told me this morning. Apparently Stephanie came to New York a few weeks ago to meet with Tina and her people at Corsair, and there was a big blowout. Stephanie stomped out, promising to sue for breach of promise. But Tina said she'd have a hard time proving that promises written on air ever existed. That's what she said—can you believe that?"

"Easily. Very interesting. Does this change your feelings about wanting to buy your book back?"

"Hell, no! The only change is that now *nobody's* going to get the big push at Corsair. I want out."

"All right. I'll send you my representation agreement tomorrow, and once I have it back from you, I'll get started trying to get the book back. I'll speak with Rafe Parker."

Salomé looked bewildered. "Representation agreement? Why do we need that? I told you—my letting you represent me is conditional on your getting Corsair to sell me my book back—for the money they've already paid me."

"I understand that," Jane said, forcing a pleasant smile, "but you have to understand that even for this conditional arrangement, I need a document stating that if I sell the book, I get my commission. No one's working without a representation agreement anymore. If I can't get the book back, we cancel."

Salomé considered this. "Okay, I guess that sounds all right."

"Good. It's been a pleasure to meet you. Have a safe trip home."

"Mm," Salomé said, and turned and walked away.

Jane shook her head. They were all, in essence, the same.

She drove home and spent the rest of Sunday playing with Nick, Winky, and Twinky. In the family room, Nick worked on a robot he was creating from his Lego Mindstorms Robotics set. The robot resembled a man wearing a large red top hat. Nick pressed a button on the remote control and it began walking forward, its mouth opening and closing.

Jane marveled that Nick had built this on his own, without instructions. "Honey, that's fantastic. It reminds me of Mr. Machine."

He frowned. "Mr. Machine? What's that?"

"A toy I had when I was very small. It was a robot you could take apart and put together again. I was too little to do it, so my dad did it for me."

She expected him to roll his eyes and make a comment about her "corny old toys," but instead he looked at her thoughtfully and said, "Mom, how come you never talk about your mom and dad?"

She gazed down at her lap. "I guess because it hurts."

"Why?"

"Because they died when I was a girl. That was a very sad time in my life." She smiled. "Someday I'll tell you about them, about my life after they died."

She thought he would demand that he tell her now, but he didn't, instead nodding and returning his attention to his robot. "Watch this, Mom," he said, and made the robot walk into Twinky, who was fast asleep on the floor. The kitten jumped up, squeaked loudly in fear, and shot from the room into the foyer.

"Nicholas! That was mean. Don't you ever do that again."

He shrugged and continued his work. On the sofa beside Jane, Winky lay curled in a ball, half asleep, trilling peacefully. Jane stroked her soft, orange-and-brown mottled fur. After Winky had become pregnant, Jane had decided to make her an indoors-only cat again. She also had had Winky— and Twinky, as soon as she was old enough— spayed.

Jane was glad to have Winky around the house more. Kenneth had given her to Nick only a month before he died. Winky had looked exactly the way Twinky looked now. Jane's veterinarian, Dr. Singh, had told her that indoor cats had a much longer life expectancy than cats allowed to go outside. That was enough for Jane. Not only did she and Kenneth love the cat, but she was a living reminder of him—a reminder Jane wanted around as long as possible.

Twinky returned, padding in from the kitchen, and keeping a wide berth around Nick and his robot, she joined Jane and Winky on the sofa. Winky began swatting at Twinky, who bounced onto Jane's lap, light as a feather. Jane laughed, remembering Winky's bizarre behavior at the cat show—a disappointing experience that, fortunately, Nick and Florence appeared to have put behind them.

*   *   *

The next morning, Jane stumbled down the small corridor that led from the back door of her offices to the reception area, her arms loaded with book proposals.

Daniel glanced up from his desk, looking handsome in a pale pink polo shirt that contrasted pleasingly with his dark skin. Lately he had taken to dressing more casually, especially on warm days when he had no lunch date in New York City. "Where did those come from?" he asked, indicating the stack of paper.

Jane dropped them onto the credenza, where she and Daniel put material to be returned. "I've had them at home for ages. They're all rejects."

"You got it," he said cheerfully, then sat looking up at her expectantly.

"What?" she asked.

"So what happened? To Tina, I mean?"

"You know about that?"

"Jane, the whole town knows about it. You should have heard people blabbing away at Whipped Cream when I dropped Ginny off. 'Was it really suicide?' 'Was she murdered?' What do you think?"

She dropped into his visitor's chair. She kept very little from Daniel. "I think she was murdered. Problem is, it's looking as if the killer could have been practically anybody in the publishing industry! This woman had a lot of enemies."

"That's what people always said. Meanest woman in publishing. What makes you think she was murdered?"

She told him what Stanley had said about the three keys.

He nodded. For a moment he sat quietly, gazing into the middle distance, pondering. "As you well know, in any murder case there are always at least several people who might have wanted to kill the victim. The crucial question is, which one had a strong enough reason to actually *do* it?"

She wrinkled her brow. "Well, *obviously.*"

He shrugged. "I just mean that in most murder cases everyone's fixated on the motive, the opportunity. But for most people, committing murder doesn't come naturally; it's a difficult thing to do. So you have to ask yourself, who wanted something *so badly* that he or she was willing to kill someone for it? And wanted *what?*"

"My, you have been giving this a lot of thought, haven't you?"

"Yes, I have." His tone was serious. "Remember, the answer almost always lies hidden in the life of the victim him- or herself."

She stared out the office's front window at the village green, its lush foliage bright in the sunshine, the white bandstand so bright it almost hurt her eyes to look at it.

"You know," she said, looking back at him, "you're absolutely right. I don't know enough about Tina. Her personal life, I mean. Oh, I knew her as a publishing person, but who was she really? When she wasn't the meanest woman in the industry."

"Did you say '*you*' don't know enough about Tina?"

"Yes."

"Meaning you're trying to solve this case?"

"Right again."

"But why? You know how Stanley feels about that."

She made a *pfoosh*ing sound. "Yes, I know how Stanley feels, and fully expect the usual lecture about not playing detective. It's easy for him to say."

"What do you mean?"

"*He*'s not one of the suspects! No," she said, heading for her office, "I'm afraid I have no choice. The police don't seem to be making any progress, so I'll have to try to find out who killed Tina—before anyone decides it was me!"

Chapter Nine

Jane doodled on her desk pad, thinking. The logical first person to talk to, of course, was Tina's husband, Ian Stein. But she had no idea how to reach him—where he lived, where he worked, even what he did for a living. She strongly doubted they were listed in the phone book, but just to make sure she called Directory Assistance. She was right. She decided to call Stanley.

"Why do you want to know that?" he asked, his tone ominous.

"I want to talk to Ian Stein."

"Why?"

"Do I need to explain everything I do to you? This *is* America."

"Yes, it is America, but if you want Ian Stein's address out of me, you're going to have to tell me what you want to talk to him about."

She blew out a gust of air. "Stanley, Stanley, Stanley, you do insist on making my life difficult.

Let me spell it out for you. I am a murder suspect. If word gets out, my career as a literary agent is over. Can you understand that?"

"Don't patronize me, Jane. Of course I understand that. But finding out who killed Tina Vale is not your job. It's a job for the police. Why don't you just leave it to us?"

"Because—forgive me, Stanley—past performance leads me to believe that if I want this job done, I have to do it myself. I'm not saying I'm definitely going to solve this case, but I can sure try. Who's solved the last four murder cases in this town? *Me!* With Winky's help, of course."

There was a long silence on the line. She waited, wincing. Finally Stanley said in a deep sigh, "I don't know yet where Tina and Ian lived. All I've got at this point is an address for Ian. You want it?"

"Uh, yes, since he's the one I've told you I want to see."

"Jane, don't use that tone with me."

"Sorry." She drummed her pencil on the desk. "The address, please."

"Nine twenty-seven Fifth Avenue."

"Thank you."

"I did not tell you that."

"Tell me what?" she asked, all innocence.

"Good-bye, Jane."

"Thank you, Stanley."

She doodled some more. She would have to go into the city to do some snooping, one of her favorite activities. She tried to get some work done. She called Harriet Green at Bantam and asked her to send her some covers of Bertha Stumpf's upcoming romance, *Shady Lady.* She read a proposal by a writer whose son went to school with Elaine Lawler's nephew. The proposal was quite poor and Jane tossed it on the reject pile.

Then she jumped up and hurried out to the reception area. Daniel was on the phone, so she jotted him a note—*Gotta run, see you tomorrow*—then ran out the back door to her car.

From her car she called Florence on her cell phone and said she had to go into New York but would be home in time for dinner. "Very good, missus. We're having my stuffed crab shells that you love."

Jane drove to the municipal parking lot at the corner of Route 46 and South Beverwyck Road in Parsippany. She had no sooner parked and gotten out of the car than a Lakeland Bus pulled up. She ran for it and was the last one on.

Forty-five minutes later, she walked out the front of the Port Authority Bus Terminal and hopped into a taxi. By the time it pulled up in front of 927 Fifth Avenue, a tony neo-Italian Renaissance building at East 74th Street, she'd devised a plan.

A gloved and uniformed doorman greeted her just inside the lobby. "May I help you, madam?"

"Yes, I'm here to see Ian Stein."

"Your name?

"Jane Stuart."

"Is Dr. Stein expecting you?"

Dr. Stein? Then he was in; good. "Yes, he is," she lied.

The doorman went to the phone, called upstairs, spoke for a moment, and returned to Jane. "I'm terribly sorry, madam, but Dr. Stein says he has no appointments this afternoon."

She let her jaw drop, forced tears to her eyes. "Oh, dear. I've come all the way in from Westchester and Dr. Stein has lost my appointment? Perhaps I could go upstairs and work things out with his secretary?"

Clearly working to maintain his composure, the doorman returned to the phone and called upstairs again. When Jane could see that he was speaking, she said, "Please mention that I'm especially concerned about the damage done by the toaster." The door man repeated this without registering any recognition of its meaning.

The doorman turned to her with a tight smile. "You may go up, madam. Twelfth floor."

When the elevator doors opened on the twelfth floor, Ian Stein was standing there waiting for her. "What do you want?" He frowned, scrutinizing her. "I know you. You're that Stuart woman. You were in our hotel suite Saturday morning."

"That's right," she said, stepping into the corridor. "I want to talk to you about your wife."

"What was it you told the doorman about a toaster?"

"I know how Tina died. In fact, I'm one of the suspects. I'm also a close friend of one of the police officers on the case, and I'm helping him out, you might say. May I talk with you in your office?"

Reluctantly he turned and led her into a suite with a sign on the door that read MANHATTAN COSMETIC SURGERY CLINIC. Then he was a plastic surgeon! No wonder Tina had still looked so good.

They sat in his office, a spacious room lined with bookcases of dark wood, with a magnificent view of Central Park.

"Now, what do you want to talk about?" he asked, settling behind his desk and motioning for her to sit.

"I'll get right to the point. I never liked your wife, and before she died I was furious at her about something she was going to do, but I certainly would never have killed her. I'm trying to find out who would have."

He gave her a baffled look, shaking his head ever so slightly so that his blond curls shook a little at his white shirt collar. "*Killed* her? My wife committed suicide."

"Drop it," Jane said. "I know about the missing key."

He nodded as if conceding a point. Jane had no desire to hurt this man, but she needed to learn all she could, and doing so meant she might *have* to hurt some people.

"Did you know that your wife was having an affair with Rafe Parker, Corsair's chairman of the board?"

If Ian was surprised, he didn't show it. He gave Jane a level stare. "I was fully aware of my wife's activities. The Parkers happened to be close friends of ours. Did you know Rafe wasn't the only one?"

"Do you mean Dario?"

His eyes widened in shock. "Dario—the Spray-Away Man?"

She nodded sadly.

"No, I didn't know about him. But it doesn't matter. You see, Tina and I had that kind of marriage."

"What kind of marriage is that?"

"A marriage of convenience, you might say. We were a good team; we looked good together. There was something between us once, a long time ago, but at the end what we had was basically a good friendship. We had a lot of fun together. I enjoyed helping her look for antique toasters. She enjoyed hearing about the saggy old women I tighten up. We were right together in so many ways." His gaze met hers. "Sexually was not one of them."

"Are you sure it didn't bother you that Tina was having affairs with other men?"

He hesitated a moment. Then he opened a drawer, took out a framed photograph, and placed it on his desk so that she could see it. It was a picture of a handsome dark-haired young man who looked as if he was in his late twenties. "No," he said, "not upset at all. As I said, sexually wasn't one of the ways we were right together."

Her gaze met his. "I understand. What about money? Did you stand to benefit financially from her death?"

"That's extremely impertinent," he said peevishly, then gave a little laugh. "I've got more money than Tina had." He indicated his office. "I'm one of the most successful cosmetic surgeons in New York City. More to the point, I'm not in Tina's will anyway. I took her out of mine long ago in favor of my friend"—he pointed to the framed photograph on his desk—"and Tina removed me from hers."

Jane nodded. "What about the missing key?"

"What about it?"

"You're certain you left yours in the ashtray by the door Saturday morning?"

"Absolutely. It's a little habit of mine—whenever I stay in a hotel, I leave the key by the door. That way I never lose it."

"And it was gone when you got back with the toaster?"

"That's right."

"Shelly threw her key at Tina when she quit, and Tina's key was still on her dresser."

"Exactly."

She was silent for a few moments, at a loss for what to ask next.

"Let me give you a tip," he said, and she looked up. "Take a harder look at Shelly. There's more to her than meets the eye."

"What do you mean?"

But he shook his head. "I'll say no more about that." He rose to see her out, walking her to the elevator. There, to Jane's surprise, he gently touched the side of her face. "You really ought to consider a lift and an eye job."

She forced a smile. "Thanks, but I like myself just as I am. I appreciate your time."

The elevator doors began to close, but she remembered something and stopped them with her hand. "Oh, Mr. Stein. Can you tell me the address of your and Tina's apartment?"

He had reached the door to his suite. He turned. "That's none of your business," he said, and went in.

Chapter Ten

Outside, Jane ambled down Fifth Avenue in the shade of the trees beside the wall separating the sidewalk from Central Park. Ian Stein's words about Shelly rang in her ears. What could he possibly have meant? She intended to find out, and decided the best place to start looking for the young woman, now that the RAT convention was over, was Corsair Publishing.

Jane had been to Corsair numerous times, most recently for meetings concerning Goddess's *My Life on Top*, which Corsair had published. The company occupied all but one floor of a building on East Twenty-second Street that had years ago been converted from a factory into elegant office space. She cabbed there and asked for Shelly Adams.

Shelly appeared almost immediately, her pretty face lighting up when she saw Jane standing in the reception area. "Well, hi!"

"Hello, Shelly. I hope you don't mind my dropping in like this."

"Of course not. I was just helping clear up Tina's things. You know, before I leave."

"I see. Shelly, may I speak with you? How about if I buy you lunch?"

"Sure," Shelly said with a puzzled shrug.

They went to a crowded pocket park beside the building, bought sandwiches from a tiny café at the back, and sat on stone benches in front of a waterfall.

"I never had a chance to congratulate you on your new relationship with Nat," Jane said, unwrapping her smoked turkey on rye.

"Thank you, Jane. I think he's very special."

"He's also extremely talented. When I read his novel, I knew this man would go far. You should ask him for a copy of the manuscript. It's a magnificent story."

"He told me most of it. It made me cry." Shelly wrinkled her brow, thinking. "It's funny about Nat. You look at him and see this little guy, kind of pudgy, with that great big mustache, and you think maybe he should be pushing a broom somewhere. Then you find out he's a pharmacist—which takes brains, right? But not only that, he's this sensitive novelist. It just proves you never know about a person just by looking at him."

"I couldn't agree more. You've got yourself a good man."

Shelly blushed. "Thanks. I guess breaking up with Terry had its good side."

"Absolutely. Rule two: Remember that there's something good in everything."

"Right!" Shelly nibbled on her sandwich.

"Shelly," Jane said, "I want to ask you about Tina and Ian's relationship."

Shelly looked at her blankly. "What about it?"

"I've spoken with Ian, and apparently theirs was a marriage in name only?"

"Yes . . ." Shelly said slowly, "that's right. Ian is—well—he's gay."

Jane nodded. "That's what he indicated. He said he and Tina were more friends than husband and wife. Would you say that's true?"

"Oh, yes. They were always laughing together, having fun. I think they really loved each other, but more like brother and sister, if you know what I mean."

"Can you think of any reason why Ian might have wanted to kill Tina?"

Shelly dropped her sandwich to her lap. "Kill her! No one killed her. What are you talking about?"

"Shelly," Jane said gently, "weren't you surprised to learn that Tina had killed herself?"

"Yes, of course I was. Who wouldn't have been?"

"No, what I mean is, that Tina specifically would have committed suicide. That she would have left a note saying she couldn't go on. *Why* couldn't she go on? What was wrong? Was she terribly unhappy about something? Could she have been secretly unhappy that her relationship with Ian wasn't more than a friendship?"

"No," Shelly said with conviction. "Tina was on top of the world."

Jane gave her a baffled look. "Then why didn't you think it was odd that she'd killed herself?"

"Because you never know with people, do you? When I was a kid I had a friend, a girl my age. We were very close, always going over to each other's house. She had everything I wanted—a big, beautiful bedroom, fancy clothes, toys, a kitten. When she got older she was the prettiest, most popular girl in high school. Then one day her mom came home from work and found Susie hanging dead in her closet. To this day no one knows why she killed herself. All we know is that up to the minute she did it, no one had the slightest idea that anything was wrong."

"Be that as it may, Tina did not kill herself."

Shelly glared at her. "What?"

Jane told her about the third key. "The police will undoubtedly interview anyone who had access to the key that went missing. That includes you, me, and a number of other people. Now, think hard—try to remember if you saw anything that might help the police figure out who took it."

"But why do *you* want to know?" Shelly asked. "Why are you asking these questions instead of the police?"

Jane made an impatient gesture. "I can't wait for the police. I can't afford to let the news of my being a suspect get out. I've got to try to solve this case before it's too late."

Shelly nodded vigorously, then looked down, thinking. "I know!" she said suddenly. "Saturday morning, before you and Nat came up to the suite, that awful Salomé Sutton came up. She and Tina had a horrendous argument. Salomé even threw a glass at Tina. Fortunately, she missed. Anyway, Salomé flounced out of the suite, and she was in such a hurry to leave that she caught her dress on the edge of the table near the door. Could she have grabbed the key then?"

"It's possible," Jane said. "Very interesting. Shelly, when I spoke with Ian, he said I should take a closer look at you, that there's more to you than meets the eye. What did he mean?"

Shelly blanched. "Ian said that?"

"Yes." Why, Jane thought again, did this young woman look so familiar?

"I . . . don't know. In what respect?"

"No idea," Jane said.

"Sorry," Shelly said. "Neither do I."

"All right," Jane said, though she wasn't sure she believed her. "Is there anything you can tell me about Tina—anything about her life that might point to her having an enemy?"

Shelly threw back her head and laughed. "An enemy! Tina was the most hated woman in publishing; *everyone* was her enemy."

"And you can't think of any problems she might have had? Not necessarily problems bad enough to make her want to commit suicide, but just . . . problems."

"Well, she was going to a therapist, but lots of people do that."

"True. Interesting. Any idea why?"

"No, no idea. She was also seeing a physical therapist."

Jane frowned. "What for?"

Shelly shook her head. "I can only guess it was for a skiing accident Tina had in Aspen last winter. She broke her ankle. But of course that would have no bearing on this."

"No," Jane agreed, and more puzzled than ever, realizing that this was all Shelly was going to tell her, she bid the young woman good-bye. "And keep in touch," Jane said, turning as she left the little park.

"Oh, I will," Shelly said. "We'll have Nat in common!"

Jane returned to her office. Remembering what Shelly had said about Salomé catching her muumuu on the table in Tina's suite, Jane found Salomé's card and called her in Rancho Santa Fe. A maid answered and put Salomé on.

"You got news for me, Jane?"

"News about what?"

"About buying my book back, what do you think?"

"No, not yet."

"Then what's up?"

"Sal, when you went up to Tina's suite on Saturday morning, you caught your dress on the table as you were leaving."

"How the hell did you know that?"

"Shelly, Tina's secretary, told me."

"Okay. So what?"

"There was a key in an ashtray on that table. Did you happen to accidentally take the key when you hit the table?"

"No . . ." Salomé replied slowly. "Why?"

"There was a key there early in the morning, and later it was gone."

"So?"

"So the police believe that whoever took the key used it later to slip into the suite and kill Tina."

"You're saying I'm a killer?" Salomé boomed.

"No, of course not."

"Yes, you are. Why else would you be asking me these questions? I don't think I can work with someone who thinks I'm a murderer, Jane. It'll kind of get in the way of our working relationship, dontcha think?"

"Sal, I'm not saying you're a murderer. I'm just saying a key went missing. If you accidentally took it, it would explain where the key went, that's all."

"Yeah, right. Well, no, Sherlock, I didn't take the key, and I didn't slip back into the suite to kill Tina, as mad as I was at her. Being angry at someone is one thing; killing her is quite another."

"You're right—I apologize for how that sounded."

"Humph. Well, call me when you have news about the manuscript, all right?"

"Certainly."

She hung up shaking her head. She'd really bungled that call. Salomé was a tough customer who needed to be handled with greater care.

She grabbed a contract from the work heap on the center of her desk and began vetting it, marking changes she wanted with yellow Post-it Notes. She was halfway through when Daniel buzzed her.

"Jane, Nat Barre is here to see you."

She went out to the reception area to greet him. She noticed immediately that he looked different—happy. He was actually smiling, that was it; she realized she'd never seen him smile before. Love will do that, she reflected.

"This is a surprise."

"Hope you don't mind."

"Not at all! Come in."

He sat in her visitor's chair. "I came to discuss my novel. Last time we strategized, Daniel was making copies to submit to new publishers. I assume that won't be necessary now."

"No," she replied uneasily, "I don't think it will.

Unless Tina shared her plans with anyone—but I don't think she did."

"Then we'll just leave things alone?"

"Yes, I think that will be best. We should wait for someone at Corsair to call and say he or she is your new editor. That's how these things usually work."

"All right." He gazed around the cluttered office. "Shelly says she saw you today."

"Yes, we had a nice lunch."

"She's a very special girl."

She smiled. "Yes, I can tell that."

"I'm so glad I decided to come out for that meeting with Tina Vale, or else I would never have met Shelly."

"That's true. Isn't life funny?"

"Yeah. I've been living with her in her apartment on the Lower East Side since the convention ended. You know," he said, leaning forward a little, "I'm in love for the first time in my life. I'm going to ask Shelly to marry me and come to Green Bay. I may even stop living with Mother."

"Well," Jane said, beaming with delight, "I'd say that's pretty wonderful. Congratulations to you both."

"Thanks, Jane. And thanks for all you've done for me—for my career, I mean. Without you believing in me, I'd be nowhere."

"Why, thank you, Nat. That's very sweet." It wasn't often Jane got thanked for her work.

He rose. "I shouldn't take up any more of your time."

"Don't be silly. It's good to hear all of this wonderful news." She walked him through the reception area to the door. "Now you be sure to give me an address and phone number where you can be reached so I can keep you apprised about your book, all right?"

"Will do. Thanks again, Jane." He said good-bye to her and Daniel and went out; they watched him cross Center Street and start slowly down one of the paths that crisscrossed the village green.

"Ah, love," Jane said with a happy sigh.

"Florence, I swear you should open a Trinidadian restaurant." Jane took another forkful of crab mixture from the shell in which it had been baked. "This is heavenly."

"Why, thank you, missus." Florence turned to Nick and frowned. Before him sat a large yellow box of Waffle Crisp cereal and a gallon of milk. "I'm afraid my stuffed crabs are not such a big hit with Master Nicholas."

He wrinkled up his nose. "Florence, I told you, I don't like to look at those yucky shells."

"Then put the cereal box in front of you, so you won't see them."

"You don't know what you're missing, Nick," Jane said, savoring the seasoned crab filling.

"Oh, Mom," Nick whined, "stop trying to get me to eat your strange grown-up food."

"That'll be quite enough of that," Jane said, and looked apologetically at Florence, who smiled.

"It's okay. When I was a little girl I didn't like it when my mother made stuffed crabs, either." She shrugged playfully. "Oh well, more for us!" And she dug into her own meal.

Within five minutes Nick had finished his bowl of Waffle Crisp. "May I please be excused?"

"Yes," Jane replied, "to finish your homework."

Groaning, Nick took up the cereal box, bowl, and spoon and stomped dramatically into the kitchen.

Florence laughed, shaking her head, then turned to Jane. "So, missus, how are you doing with your investigation?"

Jane frowned in concern. "Not very well, I'm afraid. And this silence from Stanley means the police haven't learned anything, either. This is bound to get out."

"Do you really think that would be a problem for you, missus?"

"Oh, yeah. You don't know publishing. It'll be all over the place. 'Literary Agent Suspected in Editor's Murder.'" Jane gave a sardonic laugh. "You know, it's funny. Over the years I've been an agent, there were countless times when I thought I could kill an editor. They're just so absolutely infuriating. But I never meant it. I even said it about Tina. And now she's dead, and I'm one of the people who may have done it!"

Florence gave her an arch look. "Come on now, missus. *Did* you do it?"

"Florence!"

Florence burst out laughing.

"I hardly think it's funny."

Florence forced a serious expression. "No, of course, I'm sorry. And that poor woman has died. I apologize."

"It's all right. I'm sorry to be such a downer tonight."

"Well, what *have* you learned so far?"

"Nothing helpful. Jory Mankewitz, an agent Tina betrayed on a business arrangement, said he wanted to kill her. Salomé Sutton, an author whose career Tina was going to flush down the tubes, was mad enough to kill her. Shelly Adams, Tina's meek little assistant, was angry at her because she reneged on a promise. The list goes on and on."

"So lots of people had motive, and lots of people had opportunity."

"You've been reading too many Agatha Christies."

"I do love to curl up with a detective story at night."

"Mm, well. This detective story is real, and it's going to do me great harm if either I or the police don't solve it fast."

"You know," Florence said, frowning in concentration, "when you think about it, *anyone* could have gotten into Tina's suite on Saturday. All someone would have had to do is convince the person at the front desk that he or she was staying in the suite and had lost his or her key."

Jane stared at her, then put her hand to the side of her face. "You're right." She groaned. "Which brings us back to something Daniel said. Which one of all these people wanted something so bad— something that could only be had if Tina were dead—that he or she would actually commit murder to get it? And what is that something?"

"True," Florence said thoughtfully. "I think our Daniel has been reading a lot of Agatha Christies too." She looked up, something having occurred to her. "You mentioned to me that Tina admitted she was having an affair with Rafe Parker, the chairman of the board of Corsair. If Tina told you about this, she was probably telling lots of people. Which means it may have gotten back to *Mrs.* Parker. Now *she* would have had a good motive to kill Tina Vale!"

"You're absolutely right," Jane said, jumping up and beginning to clear the table. "Thank you, Florence—for this wonderful dinner, and for being so smart."

Florence beamed. "My pleasure, missus."

Chapter Eleven

"This is a nice town," Daniel said, gazing out the car window. They had just passed a sign marked ESSEX FELLS.

"It's a borough, not a town," Jane said punctiliously.

"Well, excu-u-use me," he said, and laughed.

She looked him up and down. "You could live in this town. You're rich enough."

He looked embarrassed. Though he had grown up amid every luxury as the son of the founder of one of the country's most successful magazines, and had inherited a fortune when his father died the previous year, he lived simply and did not like to talk about money.

"Sorry," she said.

"No, you're right—Ginny says the same thing to me all the time. 'You've got the money—why not enjoy it?' She wants to know why I'm content to live in the top half of a two-family house, when I could own my own house six times its size."

"Well? Why are you?"

"I liked my life the way it was before I had Dad's money. I don't want it to change. I don't want to live that way."

"Fair enough, then! There's no law that says you have to spend money just because you've got it." Jane added under her breath, "Though *I* certainly would."

They continued south on Roseland Avenue under a canopy of gently rustling leaves through which shone the bright summer sun. Jane slowed to read a street sign on the right.

"This is it—Meriwether." She turned. "Now remember, you're my assistant."

"But I *am* your assistant."

She threw back her head and laughed. "Oh yeah, that's right!"

Meriwether Place was a narrow, winding road lined with thick-trunked oaks and maples. Set far back from the road stood some of the largest houses Jane had ever seen—sprawling colonials with wings added to wings, lots of chimneys, and multitudes of picture windows. "Unbelievable," Jane murmured.

"That one looks just like the house I grew up in," Daniel said, pointing to an especially large white one.

"Then you'll feel right at home," she said, turning onto the house's driveway. "Because this is the place."

She parked and they got out and approached the wide front porch.

"Now, how did you find out Rafe Parker lives here?" he asked.

She gave him a Cheshire Cat grin. "I have my ways."

"Come on."

"Okay," she said eagerly, stopping to look at him. "This really was a stroke of genius. I did a Google search for Rafe Parker and found an article about him. It seems that before he became chairman of Corsair a year ago, he founded a computer company called GB, which are the initials of his wife, Greta, and his middle-school-age son, Brandon. The article had been written four years ago, and Parker had just founded the company. Now, middle school is typically sixth, seventh, and eighth grade. That meant Brandon was, at that time, between eleven and thirteen. Now he would be fifteen to seventeen, which means he's in high school."

Daniel was looking at her as if she were insane.

"No, hear me out," she said. "Schools in Essex Fells are in the West Essex Regional School District, which is made up of Essex Fells, Fairfield, North Caldwell, and Roseland." She wrinkled her nose. "Rafe Parker, chairman of the board of Corsair Publishing, wouldn't like that. Too . . . diverse, too public. So I thought, what private schools would a rich guy in Essex Fells send his son to? Well, within a reasonable distance—and not counting religious or boarding schools—you have five choices: Montclair-Kimberley in Montclair, Morristown-Beard in Morristown, Newark Academy in Livingston, Pingry in Short Hills, and Saddle River Day in Saddle River. So I blocked my caller ID and just started calling them all."

"You called them? And said what?"

"That I was Mrs. Parker calling about her son, Brandon."

His eyes bugged out. "Jane, that's *illegal.*"

She made a dismissive gesture. "Oh, stop. We're investigating a *murder* here. Anyway, I bombed out in Montclair and Morristown, but I hit the jackpot in Livingston. I told the secretary I wasn't sure I was receiving all the school notices, and did she have my correct address in Essex Fells. Of course, the poor woman shouldn't have, but she recited the address: 28 Meriwether Place! And here we are!"

He look at her askance. "You're like a stalker or something."

She shrugged. "It's all in the name of—"

"What do you want?"

They jumped.

A woman had come down the front steps of the house. Jane guessed she was in her mid-forties. She was quite attractive, slim, with dark brown hair worn long, fastened at the back of her neck and running down her back. Her features were fine and even, her eyes an arresting jewel-like blue.

Jane turned to her with a smile. "Mrs. Parker? Greta Parker?"

"Yes?" she answered warily.

"How do you do. My name is Jane Stuart, and this is my assistant, Daniel Willoughby."

Mrs. Parker waited.

"We work for the police department," Jane said, and sensed Daniel stiffening at her side.

Mrs. Parker frowned. "The police department? What police department?"

"Shady Hills."

"Why? Is something wrong?"

"No," Jane said, "nothing's wrong—at least, no one in your family has been hurt. I'm sorry if I alarmed you. May we come in and speak to you?"

Mrs. Parker looked them up and down. "Do you have identification?"

"I'm sorry, I wasn't clear," Jane said. "We work for the police department, but we're not actually police officers."

"What do you want to talk to me about?"

"About Tina Vale, vice president and publisher of Corsair Publishing."

"I know who she is. I also know she's dead. Committed suicide, I understand. With a toaster!"

"Maybe," Jane said.

"What do you mean, maybe? It was a microwave oven?"

"No, what I mean is, maybe she committed suicide. The police believe she may actually have been murdered."

"Murdered? By whom?"

"That's what the police—and we—are trying to find out."

"I thought she left a note—'I can't live like this anymore,' or something like that. So how could she have been murdered?"

"The note may have been a forgery."

Mrs. Parker considered this. "Well, what does all this have to do with me?"

"Your husband is chairman of the board of Corsair, is he not?"

"Yes . . . so?"

"Please, Mrs. Parker, couldn't we sit down for a moment?"

She hesitated a moment, wringing her hands. "All right," she said at last. "Follow me."

She led them up the stairs, across the porch, and into a foyer the size of Jane's entire living room. Above their heads hung a mammoth chandelier. To the left was a formal dining room, to the right a living room filled with overstuffed furniture upholstered in green-and-gold plaid. She walked into this latter room and indicated a sofa.

"Thank you," Jane said, as she and Daniel sat down side by side.

Mrs. Parker sat down opposite them. "Now, what does this have to do with Rafe? If you're wondering how to tell me he was having an affair with Tina, don't worry about it—I already know."

"You do?" Daniel said. Jane and Mrs. Parker both looked at him in surprise.

"I've always known." Mrs. Parker frowned. "You *are* aware Rafe is no longer living here?"

"Uh, yes," Jane said.

"Then I still don't see why you're here. What does Tina's death have to do with us?"

"Well, you see, Mrs. Parker—"

"Oh, please, call me Greta."

"Thank you . . . Greta. You see, normally when a woman's husband is having an affair with a woman and that woman is murdered, one of the prime suspects is—"

"The wife!" Greta Parker tossed back her head and laughed, as if that was the funniest thing Jane could have said. "I'm sorry, but the idea of my killing Tina out of jealousy is just hysterical. As far as I was concerned, she could have him!"

Jane looked at her in puzzlement.

"I'm divorcing him," Greta explained. "I've known about the affair with Tina ever since the private detective I hired brought me back pictures of them entering and leaving her building in New York, sharing cabs, kissing in Central Park. It goes on and on."

"You wouldn't happen to know her address in New York, would you?" Jane asked.

Greta frowned. "No, I'm sorry, I don't. Wouldn't you have that?"

"Yes, of course. I'm sure we do, back at the station. So you know about the affair and are divorcing him," Jane said, eager to change the subject.

"Mm-hm. The affair plays a big role in the divorce. It's going to help me take him for half the twenty-five million dollars he's worth."

"I see," Jane said. "Greta, did you know Tina?"

She shrugged, tilted her head. "A little, not well. We met at a few company functions. Rafe and I were invited to a birthday party for her. That kind of thing."

"What did you think of her?"

Greta laughed, as if amazed to be asked such a silly question. "Why, what everyone else thought of her. She was the bitch of the western world, a monster, a ruthless animal. And those were her good points. I didn't think much of her," Greta finished quietly.

Daniel said, "Didn't you resent her when you first found out about the affair?"

"Yes, of course I did. I would have resented any woman who was having an affair with my husband. Did I kill her because of it? No. Besides, they'd been having the affair for several years. How do you think Tina ended up at Corsair? If I was going to kill her, I wouldn't have waited all these years, and I certainly wouldn't have done it that way."

"Really?" Jane said. "How *would* you have done it?"

Greta leveled a steady gaze at her. "A bullet. Just one. Right in the middle of her pretty face. I own a gun and have a license to use it, though the license doesn't cover murder, of course. It would have been done in the dark, quickly, quietly. In other words, if I had wanted her dead, she would be dead, and you would never know who did it."

Jane felt a chill run through her. "We may never know who did this."

Greta gave a careless shrug. "Does it really matter? She was a cold-blooded, horrible person, barely human. She had no redeeming qualities whatsoever. Don't you think she needed killing?"

Jane sat back a little in alarm. "I don't think anyone 'needs killing.' If I did, I wouldn't be working for the police." Out of the corner of her eye she saw Daniel turn and look at her.

Jane rose. "Thank you for your time."

Greta nodded and walked them to the door. "How did you find my address, by the way?"

"Oh, public records," Jane replied breezily, and bidding Greta Parker good-bye, led the way across the porch and down the steps toward her car.

Neither she nor Daniel spoke until they were back on Roseland Avenue, heading north. "You know," he said, "it's against the law to impersonate a police officer."

Jane giggled. "I'm sure we broke a whole bunch of laws back there. But as I was trying to say before, it's all in the name of trying to catch a murderer."

"And that makes it all right?"

"Yes," she said firmly, looking him square in the eye, "it does. The end justifies the means."

They rode in a silence for several moments.

"She's a cool customer, don't you think?" Jane said.

"Extremely. Especially the part with the gun. I'd say she's pretty cold-blooded herself."

"Mm. And I'd say that despite that business about the gun, she couldn't have cared less whether Tina Vale lived or died . . . unless she's an excellent actress." Jane turned left onto Bloomfield Avenue.

Daniel thought about this for a moment. "What about Rafe Parker himself? Couldn't he have had good reason to kill Tina? What if she had broken off their affair to take up with Dario, and Rafe found out about it and murdered her in a jealous rage? Or just killed her in an argument of some kind? I don't understand why you're not planning to speak to Rafe himself."

She turned to him with a look of surprise. "Who says I'm not?"

Jane and Daniel spent the rest of the afternoon at the office. Jane, sitting behind the mountain of papers on her desk, tried to focus on her work, but her thoughts kept drifting back to Greta Parker, an icy character if Jane had ever met one. A worthy opponent for Tina Vale? Perhaps. *A bullet. Just one. Right in the middle of her pretty face.*

Jane shivered.

Then she frowned. Greta had said that as far as she was concerned, Rafe could have Tina. Yet clearly she had envisioned murdering Tina with that one bullet.

But of course it all made sense. She had loved Rafe, had wanted him—at least enough to hire a private detective to follow him. Or had she done that simply to ensure that she got as much as possible when she divorced him? She no longer wanted him now, but was that simply because she knew she had lost him? Was that her pride talking?

Perhaps a jealous rage had once burned inside her, a rage violent enough to make her slip into Tina's suite and kill her for revenge.

Greta could easily have known that Tina would be at the Windmere over the weekend. Rafe—with whom she was no doubt still in touch, if only regarding their son—might have mentioned that Tina would be there.

Daniel buzzed her and she jumped. "Salomé Sutton on one."

Jane grimaced, remembering her conversation with Salomé the previous day.

"Jane? Are you there?" came Daniel's voice from the intercom. "You want me to say you're out?"

"No," she said at last. "I'll take it." Halfheartedly she lifted the receiver, forcing a smile. Years ago Kenneth had told her that the person at the other end of the line could always tell if you were smiling. "Hello, Sal," she said warmly. "How are you today?"

"Damn pissed off, if you want to know the truth. What was that all about yesterday—you asking me about that key?"

Jane's stomach began to twist. "I told you, Sal—I just wondered if maybe by accident you . . . took the key."

"*By accident?* Yeah," Salomé said sarcastically. "You see, I'm so big that when I bumped into that table, the key got stuck between my rolls of fat. Or maybe it fell into one of the huge pockets on my muumuu. What do you think of these theories?"

"Sal," Jane said, forcing herself to be patient, "I said I was sorry. I no longer think you had anything to do with the missing key. Shall I apologize again?"

"Yeah!"

"All right. I apologize. Now, can we move on?"

"Sure. Let's move on to what the hell are you doing to get my book back from those bastards at Corsair?"

"As of yet," Jane said honestly, "I haven't done anything."

"Really? What are you waiting for—somebody else to die?"

"These things have to be handled delicately. I'll make a phone call to the appropriate person—"

"Oh, yeah? And who is that?"

"Well, uh," Jane faltered. "Rafe Parker, I guess."

"You *guess*?"

"No—I mean yes, it's Rafe Parker. But I think after the phone call a meeting will be necessary."

"So call! Meet! Neither of us is gettin' any younger here."

"I'll do it right away, Sal."

"And let me know what happens. Immediately. You got that?"

"Yes, Sal, I've got it. I'll do it—"

But Jane was cut off by the sound of Salomé hanging up.

She looked up in wonder. Daniel appeared in the doorway. "Everything all right?" he asked with a queasy smile.

"She hung up on me!"

He made a face. "Are you sure you want to represent her?"

"I've told you—my representing her is contingent upon my getting her book back for her. And if I can do that—hell, yes. She's worth good money."

"Okay," he said, putting up his hands. "It's just that I know how you feel about Bertha Stumpf, and this Salomé seems even worse."

Jane chuckled. "No, she's not worse. They're the same, actually. They're both a pain in the ass, but they make a lot of money. So we keep them until we can't stand it another minute." She looked up suddenly, a silly, wide-eyed expression on her face. "Hey, I've got it! Salomé and Bertha are twins, separated at birth!"

He gave her a doubtful look. "Jane, why don't you call it a day? It's after five. Isn't tonight your club night?"

"Yeah, it is. It'll take my mind off Tina . . . and Salomé . . . and all of it! And you're right—the mind is going. I'm outta here." She threw two proposals and a contract into her briefcase, grabbed her purse from the credenza behind her desk, and headed for the door.

"Have a good night," she said, passing him in the doorway. "Don't stay too late. And tell Ginny I'll see her later."

"Will do," he said with a warm smile. "She's planning to ask you to help her with some sweater cables she can't get right."

"Piece o' cake!" she cried, and hurried down the short corridor at the back of the suite and out to the parking lot behind the building.

The evening promised to be glorious. The golden light of this summer late-afternoon bathed the trees surrounding the parking lot and the few cars still parked there in a tarnished, magical glow.

Jane breathed deeply and smelled rich earth and cut grass and roses. Kenneth had loved this time of day, she remembered all of a sudden, and with a sad smile she headed for her car.

On the driver's side, she opened the door of the backseat and froze, her heart skipping a beat.

It was on the seat. She couldn't make it out at first, though she knew it was something very bad. She moved closer, turning her head a little, and as she did the smell hit her, the odor of burned flesh and fur.

She clasped her hand over her mouth, unable to take her eyes off what lay on the seat.

It was a battered old toaster—scratched and dented chrome, rectangular, with rounded corners and two wide slots for toast. Except that it wasn't a slice of toast protruding from one of the slots. It was the body of a squirrel whose head, she could now see, had been jammed into the machine. The act of forcing the poor animal into the toaster had turned its head and face into an unrecognizable pulp of blood, bone, and flesh. And this pulp was blackened, burned, for whoever had done this must have plugged in the toaster. The fur on the animal's shoulders was also singed. Its legs stuck out straight, as if shot through with electricity, and its tail pointed upwards, like a stiff bristle brush.

Then she saw the note lying on the seat next to this spectacle. It was a small square of white paper, one corner of which was stained with the squirrel's blood. Knowing she shouldn't, but unable to stop herself, she reached out and gingerly pulled the paper toward her. There was writing on it—lines in

shaky block lettering—as if, it occurred to Jane,
whoever had written it was right-handed but had
used his left hand, or vice versa. It said:

> MIND YOUR OWN BUSINESS
> OR YOU WILL BE NUMBER THREE.

She looked again at the crushed squirrel head,
and bile rose in her throat. Dropping her purse
and briefcase, she ran back to the door of the building and banged on the window.

Within moments Daniel appeared, a look of alarm
on his face. "What happened?"

"It's awful," she said, her hand still over her
mouth. She grabbed his wrist and led him quickly
to her car, pointing. He glanced at her, then peered
in, an expression of revulsion coming over his face.

"Oh," he said sickly, slowly moving closer. "What
on earth—?" Then he saw the note on the seat,
turned his head a little, and read it. He looked at
Jane, wide-eyed. "We'd better call Stanley."

"Yes," she said, and at that exact moment her
cell phone rang in her purse. "Maybe this is him."
She wrenched open the purse and yanked out the
phone. *"Stanley?"*

"No, just me, missus," came Florence's cheery
voice. "Just wondering when you'll be home. Nick
is very hungry, and also don't forget you have your
knitting club meeting tonight. I've made you some
of my famous coconut bread for you to take . . .
Missus? Are you there?"

"Yes, Florence. There's—something has happened. I'll be home as soon as I can."

"Are you all right?" Florence asked in alarm.

"Yes, I'm fine, but I have to call Stanley." She switched off the phone, then switched it back on again and punched out Stanley's number. He answered on the third ring.

"Oh, Stanley," she said, "you have to come to my office—the parking lot, I mean, in back. Come right away."

"Jane, what's going on? Are you okay? What happened?"

"I'm fine. Just come, will you?"

"I'll be right there."

"What on earth . . . ?" Stanley said, leaning into the car. Abruptly he turned and looked at Jane and Daniel. "It's a squirrel."

"We *know* it's a squirrel, Stanley." She shook her head. "What kind of sick monster would do such a thing?"

He looked at her as if she were mentally lacking. "The same sick monster who threw the toaster into Tina Vale's bathtub. Now do you see," he went on in a scolding tone, "why I'm always telling you to leave police work to the police?"

"Why?" she demanded angrily. "So I won't get toasted squirrels left on my backseat?"

"No," he snapped back, "so you won't get yourself killed. Whoever murdered Tina knows you're poking around—"

"*Obviously.*"

"—and wants you to stop."

"Well I won't," she said petulantly. "Because right now I'm a suspect, not a victim, and until you blockheads figure out who killed Tina—and did this—I'm going to keep on poking around." She looked him straight in his dark brown eyes. "And you can't stop me!"

For a second he just stared at her. He opened his mouth, then closed it again and gave a great shrug as if admitting defeat. "I'll get this mess out of your car, clean it up for you."

"Thank you," she said, softening, and gave him a grateful smile.

He nodded. "Daniel, can you drive Jane home?"

"Of course." Daniel bent over and picked up her purse and briefcase, then took her by the arm. "Come on, Jane. Sit for a minute in my car. I'll get my stuff and be right back."

She got into Daniel's car and watched him go into the building. A few parking spaces away, Stanley stood by the open door of his own car, speaking into his police radio.

Chapter Twelve

"A toasted squirrel!" Florence said in horror, then turned sharply when Nick entered the kitchen.

"What'd you say?" he asked, looking bewildered.

"Nothing," Jane said quickly. "I saw a squirrel."

He gave her a strange look. "So?"

Florence blurted out, "So it was a big one, right, missus? A big squirrel."

Nick sat down at the kitchen table, his eyes on the two women. "A big squirrel, huh?" He raised and lowered his brows. "I'd say you two are nuts!"

Florence burst out laughing; it sounded very false to Jane, which of course it was.

"That we are, little mister, that we are," Florence said. "Now, have you washed your hands?"

"Yes. Mom, why did Daniel drive you home? Where's your car?"

"In the shop," she answered quickly. "It was acting up on me today, so I left it at the garage and asked Daniel for a ride."

"Mm," he said skeptically, but dinner—not to mention Winky and Twinky purring on the seat beside him—distracted him, and the subject of the squirrel was not brought up again.

After dinner, Nick went upstairs to play on his computer.

"Missus!" Florence hissed as soon as Nick was gone. "What are you going to do?"

Jane's face grew puzzled. "About what?"

"About the murderer!" Florence said in exasperation. "You must stop your detective-playing. You saw the note. Or you are the next toast!"

"Nonsense," Jane said airily. "I have no intention of stopping."

"But *why?*"

"Because that awful thing in the back of my car tells me I'm getting close to figuring this out. Why would I stop *now?*"

"Oh, missus," Florence said in bleak resignation, and handed her a plate of sliced coconut bread covered in Saran Wrap.

"Thanks." Jane gave her a cheery smile. "Smells yummy. I appreciate your making it. Mind if I use your car?"

"I was going to visit my friend Noni tonight. May I give you a ride?"

"That would be great," Jane said.

Slowly, as if unconsciously, Florence shook her head from side to side.

Florence negotiated the twists and turns of narrow Plunkett Lane. Soon she was turning right, pulling up the long driveway of Hydrangea House. She stopped the car in front of the sprawling old inn. "Don't forget the coconut bread," she said as Jane got out.

"I won't," Jane replied, sounding as if nothing had happened that afternoon. She took the plate of cake from the backseat, then grabbed her knitting bag from the floor. "Thanks for the ride. Remember, not a word to Noni or anyone else. And if anyone asks, my car's in the shop."

"Very well, missus," Florence said with a sigh. "Call me at Noni's when you're ready to go home."

It was a lovely, balmy evening with the scent of honeysuckle in the air. Tonight the meeting of the Defarge Club, Jane's knitting group, would take place on the inn's wide front porch.

Seated on white wicker chairs, loveseats, and sofas fitted with bright floral cushions, the ladies settled themselves and their knitting bags and took peeks at their snack, which Jane had set down on the coffee table.

"Have we got enough light?" Louise Zabriskie asked, taking her seat at the head of the group. "I put extra lamps out here this afternoon—we don't want to strain our eyes."

Louise and her husband, Ernie, owned the sprawling old Victorian inn, the only such establishment in Shady Hills. Louise was a small, birdlike woman, sharp-featured with close-cropped brown hair. Tonight she wore a sensible navy skirt, white blouse, and navy cardigan, the one she always wore when they held the knitting club meetings outside.

"Jane doesn't need light," said Ginny Williams with a laugh. She sat on one of the loveseats beside

Jane. Ginny was Jane's best friend of all the women in the group. A waitress at Whipped Cream, the café across the green from Jane's office, she was also Daniel's girlfriend.

Jane turned to her. "What do you mean?"

Ginny's smile lit up her pixieish face. "You knit so fast you don't even see what you're doing. I think you could knit in the dark!"

It was true. Jane was the fastest knitter in the group, but not because she tried to be. It just came naturally to her. It was also, she found, a wonderful way to relax. She always looked forward to the easy companionship of the women in the club.

"The heck with that," came the deep, brisk voice of Doris Conway, who sat, thin and stooped, in the wicker chair opposite Louise's. Doris's eyes sparkled in the dim light. "Jane," she said hungrily, "tell us about your *murder.*"

"What? What murder?" Rhoda Kagan, sitting opposite Jane, was an attractive, well-tended forty-one, with gently waving variegated blond hair to her shoulders and bright blue eyes. Divorced two years now from David the philandering dentist, she was dating a wonderful man named Adam Forrest.

"It's not *my* murder," Jane said, pulling her latest project—a pine green alpaca pullover she'd found in *Vogue Knitting*—from her knitting bag. "And it's a long story . . ."

"We like long stories," said Penny Powell in her whispery voice. The previous fall, Penny had effected an amazing transformation in her life and marriage. She had told her chauvinistic husband, Alan, that if he didn't change and help her take care of their infant daughter, Rebecca, she would leave him. Alan, to everyone's amazement, *had* changed, and so had Penny. She no longer hid behind curtains of hair; now she wore it in a stylish short cut. She no longer sat sunk into her chair as if she wished she could disappear; now she sat up straight, unafraid to speak or be seen. She watched Jane, waiting.

Jane realized that withholding the story of Tina's murder was hopeless. Her fingers flying as she knit away on her sweater, she launched into the story.

A good twenty minutes later, she finished up: "And so you see why one of the suspects, to my great horror, is *me!*"

Louise, working on a set of crocheted doilies for the chairs in the inn's living room (there had been considerable discussion as to whether crocheting should be allowed in the knitting club), made a harrumphing sound. "She wouldn't have been electrocuted if the Windmere had GFI outlets. It's shameful, a place like that."

"What on earth is a GFI outlet?" Rhoda asked.

"I know," Penny said. "Ground fault interrupter. It's that special outlet they put in kitchens and bathrooms—anyplace there's water—so you can't get electrocuted."

"Of course they don't have them at the Windmere," Doris said, leaning forward to grab a hunk of coconut bread. "I'm telling you, Jane, this Florence is an absolute treasure. She should open a restaurant." She bit into the sweet, fragrant bread and closed her eyes, savoring it.

"Why don't they have these GFIs at the Windmere?" Ginny asked, her complicated cables in a heap on her lap.

"Because," Doris said, her mouth full, "it's an old place, built long before GFI outlets were required by law, and that crafty bastard who owns the place has been greasing the palm of the inspector so that he hasn't been forced to bring the place up to code." She shook her head and made a clucking sound. "This village isn't called Shady Hills for nothing."

"What crafty bastard?" Louise asked.

"Sammy Archer. I'm sure I've talked about him. I taught him." Doris had been a schoolteacher before her retirement years ago. "Never liked that boy. Always working the angles."

"Well, he should be reported," Louise said. "I'm sure there's going to be a heck of a lawsuit over this. If this Sammy had had the GFIs, Tina wouldn't have died."

"Yes, she would," Rhoda said easily, taking a slice of coconut bread. "The murderer would have found another way. So," she said, looking at Jane with a sparkle in her blue eyes, "why'd you do it?"

They all burst into laughter—except for Jane.

"Is that supposed to be funny? I'm running all over creation trying to figure out who *did* do this, so that my name and reputation aren't dragged through the mud of publishing, and you're making light of it? Thanks, Rhoda."

Rhoda curled out her lower lip in a faux pout. "I'm sorry, Jane. I was just making a joke. Besides, we all know *you* didn't do it, or else you wouldn't have found that toasted squirrel in your car this afternoon. Whoever did *that* is the killer." She shivered, then frowned in thought. "You know, Jane, you really should stop this snooping around, or this maniac will find some way to toast you!"

Jane gave her a kind smile. "I appreciate your concern, Rhoda, and I promise I'll be very careful."

"Evening, ladies." Ernie, Louise's husband, had appeared on the porch. Jane looked at him and did a double take. He must have put on twenty pounds since she'd last seen him. His belly strained against the fabric of his scarlet polo shirt.

They all greeted him politely. Jane forced a smile. She had never liked Ernie much. He was a womanizer whose antics had several times threatened to destroy his marriage. Lord only knew what women saw in him. But Louise loved him dearly, which was why they were still married after all these years, still running Hydrangea House together.

"So what's up?" he asked, standing behind his wife's chair.

"We're talking about the murder at the Windmere," Penny told him.

"Murder?" Ernie said avidly, his eyes wide behind his heavy black-framed glasses. "You mean that Vale woman? But she committed suicide."

The ladies all shook their heads pityingly.

"You're just not in the know, Ernie," Rhoda said. "Jane has just been telling us she was murdered."

"Murder! Wow," he said with a smile, as if this were a new form of entertainment in town.

A black Chevy Suburban pulled up the inn's long drive, circled in front of the porch, and parked in the line of cars to the right. An elderly man got out, a newspaper under his arm, and made his way creakily up to the porch.

"Evening, all," he said.

"Hello, Mr. Hammond," Louise said. "Did you have a nice day?"

"Lovely, just lovely." He stopped to look at the ladies busily knitting. "Have you seen the paper? Big happenings in Shady Hills."

They all looked up as he unfolded his copy of the *New York Post*. As Jane read the bold headline her stomach tied itself in a tight knot.

TINA GETS TOASTED

HATED PUBLISHER'S DEATH SUICIDE—OR JUSTICE?

"Oh, no," Jane said with a groan, and put her head in her hands. She looked up. "Mr. Hammond, does the story name any suspects?"

"No," he replied, frowning in thought, "don't think so." He smiled. "Bet somethin' like this hasn't happened in this town for a long time."

"Actually," Rhoda said casually, "it has. At the rate of one a year, sometimes two. Right, Jane?"

Jane glared at her reprimandingly.

Mr. Hammond's glance darted about in alarm; then he nodded a quick good-bye and hurried into the inn. Ernie, laughing silently, watched him go inside.

"Oh, you meanies," Louise said with a scolding smirk. "Scared the poor old man half to death."

"But it's true!" Rhoda said.

"I know it's true, but you didn't have to tell him. Doesn't exactly help my business."

Doris looked up. "You're just pissed off because you made bids for those two events and didn't get them," she said matter-of-factly.

Louise stared at her, saying nothing.

"What does she mean?" Ginny asked.

Louise took a deep breath and turned to her. "She's right. I did make bids on the cat show and the romance convention, but the Windmere got both. I don't know how they were able to accommodate both events at the same time."

"They almost weren't," Jane said with a laugh, remembering the fight over Conference Room D.

Ernie, still standing behind Louise, said, "Louise is worried because business is a bit down." He kissed the top of her head. "But as I told you, honey, business is down everywhere. Things will pick up."

She put her hand over his on her shoulder. "I know. You're right, I suppose."

Rhoda plunked down her knitting needles and sat up straight. "Let's change the subject," she said brightly. "Jane, tell us about all the suspects."

Jane gave her a look of dismay. "I thought we were changing the subject."

"We are—away from business here at the inn. We want to hear more about this murder, don't we, girls?"

They all eagerly agreed.

"Damn straight," Doris said.

And so Jane ran through the list of suspects, finishing up with her and Daniel's visit to Greta Parker that morning.

"It's obviously the husband," Ginny pronounced when Jane had finished.

They all turned to her.

"What makes you say that?" Jane asked.

"Don't you see? That business about his being gay is a cover! In truth, he's still madly in love with Tina, but she's been having affair after affair."

Ginny shut her eyes melodramatically. "He can't take it anymore. He hates her for not returning his love. If he can't have her, no one will. So he walks into the bathroom while she's in the tub, plugs in the toaster, pretending to want to show her how it works, and drops it into the water. ZAP!"

They all jumped.

Jane was watching her friend thoughtfully. "You know, Ginny, you may have something there. How do we really know he's gay, that he was content to have a platonic relationship with Tina? I'll definitely follow up on that. Thanks!"

"Hey," Ginny said, "I helped with the investigation, too!"

"Oh, brother," Doris mumbled.

"Well, what's *your* theory, Doris?" Rhoda asked.

"Don't have one. Don't care."

"You don't care?" Rhoda said. "A woman has been murdered, and our Jane is one of the suspects."

Doris said, "Of course I care about you, Jane. But this woman sounds as if she was Satan himself—or herself. As Mrs. Parker said, she needed killin'."

"Doris!" Penny cried.

Doris shrugged, concentrating on the difficult pattern of the shawl she was knitting for a friend at the village's senior center, where she volunteered two days a week. "I call 'em as I see 'em."

"You certainly do," Louise said, watching her with something close to horror. Her face brightened. "I think we need another subject change." She turned to Jane. "Do you know, I believe I saw your Mr. Barre at the library on Saturday."

Jane smiled. "Yes, he said he was going there to do some research for his next book."

"I was browsing the shelves, looking for something interesting to read, and I overheard a man speaking to the reference librarian—you know, that young woman with the unfortunate mole."

"What did the man look like?" Jane asked. "The one you thought was Nat."

"Medium height, stocky, bushy mustache, needed a haircut. Oh, and he was wearing the most inappropriate heavy tweed sport jacket."

"That was Nat."

"He was asking to see a book—now what was it called? Three letters." Louise frowned. "The *RDP?*"

"Was it the *PDR?*" Doris asked.

"Yes! That was it. What is that?"

"*Physicians' Desk Reference,*" Doris replied. "It's the classic drug reference book."

"Why would he want that?" Rhoda asked.

"He is a pharmacist," Jane told her. "At least he was before I sold his novel."

Louise looked irritated. "I can tell you what he wanted it for, if you'll all stop interrupting and let me finish."

"Temper, temper," Doris murmured, without looking up.

Louise ignored this. "Anyway, he told the librarian he was a novelist and that she should look for his new book, which with any luck would be published in the spring of next year. He said it was called *The Blue Palomino.*"

Jane chuckled. "It's *palindrome. The Blue Palindrome.*"

"Stupid title," Doris said.

Louise went on, "The librarian got all excited and said she loved meeting authors. Really, she fawned all over him. It was quite embarrassing. She asked him if he needed this drug book for research for his next novel, and he said yes, and showed her that he had his laptop computer set up in one of the carrels. At any rate, she got him the book and he took it to his seat and started leafing through it."

Doris looked at Louise. "Louise, what was the point of that story?"

Louise's mouth opened in surprise. "I just thought it was an interesting coincidence that I should see one of Jane's authors, that's all."

"Well, you were wrong," Doris said matter-of-factly. "Next time you eavesdrop, could you pick up something a bit juicier?"

"Oh, you're all impossible," Louise blustered, and returned her attention to her crocheting.

Doris stopped knitting and stuffed her needles and shawl into her knitting bag. "Can't do any more. Eyes too tired. Louise, having our meetings outside isn't going to work unless you give us more light than this."

"Sorry, Doris," Louise replied. "I did ask you all if there was enough light. I'll speak to Ernie."

Doris nodded. "Jane, when are you seeing Rafe Parker?"

They all looked at her.

Jane said, "How did you know I'm going to see him?"

"Well, I'd hope you would, if you had a brain—which I know you do, unlike some people around here. If Rafe—silly, pretentious name, by the way—"

"I believe it's short for Raphael," Penny put in.

"I know, Penny," Doris said with a groan. "*As I*

was saying, if Rafe knew his wife was planning to sue him for divorce and that he stood to lose half his fortune, and that Tina was shooting her mouth off to everyone including the milkman about her affair with him—after all, Jane, she told you, and she barely knew you—then he may have murdered Tina to shut her up . . . to eliminate the most dangerous evidence of his affair—his mistress!"

"Interesting," Rhoda said thoughtfully.

"You bet it is," Doris said. "'Course, there are other reasons he could have killed her. Lovers' quarrel. . . . He could have been angry that she was seeing other men. She may have been blackmailing him—who knows? After all, she was now working closely with him. Maybe she'd picked up some secrets he couldn't allow to get out. If he's anything like these pigs stealing money from their own companies—Enron, Tyco, WorldCom"—she shook her head sorrowfully—"then he'd have had very good reason to commit murder."

"Good points, Doris," Jane said. "I do intend to speak to him."

"Surprised you haven't already," Doris said, and bending forward, she snatched another slice of coconut bread and bit into it with gusto. "A treasure, Jane, a treasure!"

Chapter Thirteen

The following morning Jane sat at her desk, tapping her pencil on her knee, listening to Daniel talking on the phone with Tanya Selman, one of his clients, and waiting for him to finish. At last she heard him say good-bye and hang up, and hurried out to the reception area.

"I need you to spy for me."

He frowned as if he hadn't heard her correctly. "I beg your pardon?"

"Spy. For me. Are you willing?"

"What are you talking about?"

She dropped into the chair in front of his desk. "What if Ian was lying? What if he's not gay, doesn't have a boyfriend? Who knows who that young man was in the photo? It could have been his nephew. What I'm trying to say is, what if it was only Tina who wanted a platonic relationship; what if he still wanted to be her husband in the traditional sense? Her various love affairs would have driven him wild."

"And he would have killed her out of jealousy?"

Jane remembered Ginny's dramatic performance at the Defarge Club meeting the previous evening. "If I can't have her, no one will!"

Daniel nodded pensively. "Yes, could be something there."

"*Exactamente!* So we need to find out. If Ian is really gay, I mean."

"But how?"

"The simplest way is to follow him, see if he meets up with this young man, watch them."

"You want me to *follow* him? What if the young man goes to Ian's building?"

"I don't think that would happen. I got the feeling from the fact that Ian had the photograph hidden in his desk drawer that he's not out of the closet—at least not in his professional life. He's a hugely successful plastic surgeon—a lot of the people he works on are older women. He knows he's attractive to many of them—which doesn't hurt business—and that if they knew he was gay, that attraction might be gone. Also, older people aren't always as open-minded as others about homosexuality. He knows he might lose patients if it were known he was gay. So, no"—she shook her head—"I doubt his boyfriend would go to Ian's office. Ian would meet him."

Daniel slouched back in his chair, as if sensing the futility of arguing with Jane any further. "All right," he said with a sigh, "what do you want me to do?"

"Okay," she said eagerly, leaning forward with her elbows on the desk. "First I want you to call his office, making believe you're a prospective patient trying to make an appointment for a consultation."

"For what?"

"Oh, I don't know—a nose job."

"Okay."

"Get the soonest day you can but tell his secretary you want to come as late as possible—the last appointment of the day—because you live out here in New Jersey and you work. In other words, get her to tell you when Ian finishes for the day."

"And make an appointment?"

"Sure—but give a fake name, fake address, et cetera. You'll never show up, of course."

"Then what?"

"On the day of your appointment, I want you to start watching Ian's building when he's finished for the day. It'll be easy because he's on Seventy-fourth Street near Fifth Avenue. You can sit on a bench across Fifth—you'll be near the Central Park wall—and just watch. That way the doorman won't see you. When Ian comes out, follow him. I want to know where he goes, who he meets with. Got it?"

He nodded. "When am I supposed to do this?"

"Now, ASAP. Call and make the appointment."

Shaking his head, he picked up the phone, then stopped. "Hey, wait a minute. I don't know what this Stein looks like."

Jane, heading into her office, stopped. "You're right." She thought for a moment. "Do me a favor. Get on the Internet and see if he's got a Web site with his picture."

"Okay," he said with a sigh, and Jane continued into her office and sat down at her desk. She noticed that Daniel had added some papers to the heap, which seemed a bit higher than before, perhaps even in danger of collapsing to the right, but she couldn't deal with that now. She had to figure out a way to see Rafe Parker.

She'd begin by simply calling and see where that got her. She dialed Corsair and asked for him. The phone was answered by his secretary, Adele, whom Jane knew over the phone but had never met, just as she had never met Parker himself.

Adele sounded surprised to hear from Jane. "I was going to call you," she said.

"You were? Why?"

"Mr. Parker would like to set up a lunch date."

Jane frowned into the phone. "He would? Why?"

"I really wouldn't know, Mrs. Stuart."

"Well, I need to see him, too, so yes, let's make a date, and the sooner the better."

"All right, let me check his schedule. Hold, please."

Jane waited, carefully pulling pink message slips out of the heap, glancing at them, and tossing them onto the top. Someday she really would have to do something about this mess. Someday.

Adele came back on. "Mrs. Stuart, you wouldn't by any chance be available today, would you?"

"Today? Why is he in such a rush?"

"I really—"

"I know, you really wouldn't know. Let me check my schedule." Jane pretended to be leafing through her appointment book. "Why, yes, as it happens, I can come in today."

"Great. Mr. Parker usually lunches at the Grill Room at The Four Seasons. Will that be all right?"

Jane wasn't a big fan of The Four Seasons, but that didn't matter. "Yes, that will be fine."

"Twelve-thirty."

"Perfect. I'll see him there."

On her way out of the office she saw a printed-out photograph on Daniel's desk and picked it up.

"Is that him?" he asked.

"That's him," she replied, looking down at the attractive face surrounded by boyishly curly blond hair. "Where'd you find it?"

"On his Web site, like you said."

"Good work," she said, and saluted. "I'll await your report."

At the Grill Room at The Four Seasons, Jane was shown to one of the half-round tufted brown leather banquettes against one of the walls of gold-toned hardwood. Rafe Parker smiled and rose to greet her.

He wasn't at all what she had expected. She had expected a tall, urbane, handsome man, a fitting counterpart to the coolly elegant Tina. In reality, Rafe Parker was rather short, neither thin nor fat, with thinning black hair combed straight back and a pencil-thin black mustache. His brown eyes gleamed. "A pleasure to meet you at last."

His handshake was warm and firm. "Thank you," she said, sliding behind the table. "I'm so glad to meet you, too. Let me say first how sorry I am about Tina."

His face grew solemn. "Thank you. Thank you very much. A terrible loss for Corsair. And so young. Cut down in her prime."

Oh, brother. "True, so true." She looked at him curiously. "How old was she, exactly?"

"Forty-five."

No way! Jane had known since she and Tina worked together at Silver and Payne that Tina was twelve years older than Jane, who was now forty. That meant Tina was fifty-two when she died. Jane had to admit Tina hadn't looked fifty-two—thanks, no doubt, to her husband's surgical talents.

"Very sad," she said.

Their waiter arrived with menus, and Rafe ordered a bottle of mineral water for the table.

"Adele said you wanted to see me about something?" Jane said pleasantly.

"Uh, yes, I did, Jane. I can't believe we haven't met before this, given the huge success of *My Life on Top.*"

So that was it—Goddess's book. Jane knew it was selling extraordinarily well, but this meant it was selling even better than she had suspected. He wanted a follow-up.

"I'm so pleased about that," she said. "But of course Goddess is a natural. Everybody in the world loves her."

"That's for sure. We've sold foreign rights up the wazoo. How much longer is her show scheduled to run, do you know?"

Goddess's one-woman Broadway show, *Goddess of Love,* had been one of the hottest tickets in town for more than a year and a half. "Probably forever!" Jane replied, laughing.

"I can believe it. She's a phenomenon. Any more films in the works?"

Jane had recently spoken to Goddess and received a full report on the pop star's work plans. "As a matter of fact, yes. A movie called *Taking It*— it's supposed to start filming this fall. She'll have to take a break from *Goddess of Love,* of course."

"*Taking It?* I thought she already made a movie with that title."

"No, that was *Doing It.*"

"Ah! I love it. Who else is in it?"

"Denzel Washington and Ben Stiller."

"Hmm." He frowned thoughtfully, watching the waiter fill their glasses with water. "Odd combination. But it will no doubt break records."

"No doubt," she said, and raised her glass. "Here's to the continued success of *My Life on Top.*"

He clinked his glass to hers, keeping those soulful brown eyes fixed on her. "So," he said casually, putting down his glass, "have you sounded out your client on the subject of doing a sequel?"

Inwardly she smiled. "A sequel? Actually, no. Isn't it a little early to be talking about that?"

"I don't think so. Once we decide on a concept and find the right ghost, get the thing written, it'll be a good year from now before we publish. We published *My Life on Top* last month. So it would be thirteen months between books."

"True," she conceded, then put on a concerned face. "I don't know if it will happen, though, Rafe."

He looked crestfallen. "Why not?"

"Money was a big problem the first time around. Jack Layton knew that Goddess wanted Holly Griffin to have the book, to be her editor, and he took advantage of that fact by making me a lowball offer I was forced to accept." She shook her head. "Holly's gone now, and Goddess is smarter, too."

"Absolutely," he said, nodding quickly. "Absolutely. Jack Layton's gone, too, thank heavens. So we can start fresh. What did we pay you for the first one?"

"A million-five."

"Really!" He looked revolted. "No wonder you feel as you do. I can't believe Jack did that to you. What were you looking for?"

"As I recall, five million."

"Would you take that for the sequel?"

"Assuming Goddess would be willing to do one . . . no."

"No?" He gulped.

"No."

"What *are* you looking for?"

"Ten million."

He choked on his mineral water. "That's a bit higher than I had in mind."

"Oh? And what did you have in mind?"

He looked her straight in the eye. "Seven and a half million dollars, world rights."

"Interesting," she said. "Is that an official offer?"

"Sure is."

She smiled, taking up her menu. "I'll be delighted to present it to my client."

"Wonderful," he said, quickly setting down his menu. He looked at her, brows creased. "Adele said there was something you wanted to talk to me about. Was it Goddess?"

"No. Actually, it was Tina."

"Tina?"

She nodded, putting down her menu. "She told me you and she were having an affair."

His jaw dropped. "She told you that?"

"Isn't it true?"

He hesitated, playing with his silver. "Yes, it's true," he blurted out at last, "but I can't see why she would have told you that. Besides, what does it have to do with anything? That was a private matter between Tina and me, and she's gone now, poor soul."

"Yes, she's gone now. That's what I wanted to talk about."

"What do you mean?"

"Rafe, are you aware that the police believe Tina was murdered?"

"Murdered!"

"Yes. They believe someone stole a key to her suite at the hotel, slipped in, and killed her, leaving a forged suicide note."

"I can't believe that. Why would anyone want to kill Tina?"

Jane burst out laughing. "Apparently you saw a different side of Tina than the rest of the world."

"What does that mean?"

"Oh, come off it, Rafe. She was a bitch! She was the most detested person in the entire publishing industry. Forgive me for saying so, but I can't even begin to imagine how you could have had an affair with her." She shuddered. "It must have been like making love to a rattlesnake."

Unexpectedly, he gave her a sly smile. "Don't knock it till you've tried it."

"And what is *that* supposed to mean?"

"Of course I didn't see her tough business side. We were lovers, for Pete's sake. But she was never a pushover, always a tigress, I'll say that for poor Tina."

"Does it make you angry that she told me about your affair? Was she in the habit of telling virtual strangers about it?"

He brooded a moment. "I don't know why she was so indiscreet. I begged her to keep her mouth shut, but no one could tell Tina Vale what to do.

Yes, I could have wrung her lovely neck for being such a blabbermouth."

"Why? Because it made you more vulnerable in your upcoming divorce?"

"How do you know about that?"

"I know more than you think, Rafe. Greta intends to take you to the cleaners and back again. Wouldn't it have been better for you to have Tina and her big mouth out of the picture?"

He gaped at her, making high squeaking noises. "Are you saying I murdered Tina?"

"I'm saying you could have."

"Wait a minute. What business is Tina's murder of yours? What are you doing, playing detective? She was no friend of yours. Why are you meddling in this?"

"Because I saw Tina in her suite the morning of the day she died, and I am a suspect in her murder. It's only a matter of time before that news gets out and ruins my career—unless I find out who really killed her, and fast."

Gazing at her, he smiled a little and nodded. "I know why you went to see her, I remember now. Last Friday, Tina mentioned to me that she was going to some godforsaken burg to get some silly award, and that to make things worse, you had insisted on meeting with her to talk about that awful novel you sold her."

Jane froze. "What novel?"

"*The Blue Popsicle,* I don't know. Tina said the author revised it and it was horrendous. She was rejecting it."

So Tina had mentioned this to at least one other person at Corsair. Jane decided not to get into Tina's vendetta against her over Kenneth, or the fact that Tina hadn't even read Nat's revised manuscript.

"And are you rejecting it?" she asked.

"I don't know," he said, as if such trivial matters were beneath him. "When I get a new publisher in to replace Tina, I'll let her decide."

"I see. How do you know your new publisher will be female?"

He rolled his eyes. "It's just a manner of speaking. I meant whoever it is." He shook his head in wonder. "I can't believe you think I could have killed Tina."

"Stranger things have happened, Rafe. You stand to lose twelve and a half million dollars when Greta is finished with you. People have killed for a lot less."

"It's funny," he marveled. "You act as if you've met her."

"I have."

He stared at her in shock. "You have? When? Where?"

"At your house in Essex Fells. Lovely home, by the way. Too bad you're not living in it anymore."

"Why did Greta speak to you?"

Jane shrugged.

"I know why. To get back at me. She hates me. She's crazy, you know."

"What do you mean? She seemed perfectly sane to me."

He laughed. "She always does. But she's been institutionalized. She's got a paranoid personality disorder. Funniest thing was, she thought I was having affairs for years before I really was. Finally I couldn't take it anymore and I left. Her doctors don't blame me—they can't believe I put up with her as long as I did. I fully expect to get custody of our son."

"Brandon."

"How do you know his name?"

Again she just shrugged.

He smiled rakishly, sliding a little closer to her on the banquette. "What are you," he said in a low, sexy voice, "some kind of kinky stalker?"

Would he tell her more if she played his game? She winked at him. "If you want me to be." She growled, tossed her head.

His gaze traveled over her. "I love that red hair."

"Auburn."

"Pardon?"

"Auburn. My hair is auburn."

"Well, it's very sexy."

"Thank you."

The waiter returned, ready to take their orders.

"I don't know about you," Rafe said to Jane, "but I'm not very hungry today. Maybe we should just go back to my office." He lifted an eyebrow meaningfully.

"Sounds like a plan," she purred.

Rafe turned to the waiter. "I'm sorry, but we won't be eating today."

"That's quite all right, Mr. Parker. We'll see you again soon."

"Just put the water on my tab."

"Excellent."

They left the restaurant together and took a taxi down Park Avenue to Corsair's offices on East Twenty-second Street.

Upstairs, Rafe introduced Jane to Adele, a

plump motherly woman with soft blond hair. Then
he led the way into his huge corner office, closing
the door behind him.

Jane started to sit in the chair facing Rafe's desk,
but he went instead to an intimate sitting area in
an alcove far to one side of the room. He sat down
on a black leather sofa and patted the cushion beside him. Jane walked over and slid into place beside him.

"This is very nice," she said, looking around.

"Mm, thanks. You're very nice, too."

She turned to him to find him only inches away,
gazing sheeplike into her eyes.

"Tell me, Rafe," she said into his face. "Did it
bother you that Tina was seeing other men while
she was seeing you?"

That shattered the mood a bit.

He drew back, frowning. "Are we still talking
about that?"

"I'm just curious. I think it's kind of—I don't
know—kinky. You know, the idea of different
men at the same time . . ." She gave a little shrug
and winked at him playfully.

His eyes grew large. "You're into that? Hm, now
that can be arranged."

"Well, did it?"

"Did what?"

"Did it bother you? You know, that Tina was seeing Dario and whoever else she was seeing?"

"No," he said softly, "it didn't bother me that
she was sleeping with Dario and our art director
and that jerk over at Simon & Schuster and the
mailman. You know why? Because I was sleeping
with lots of women! Now," he said, nestling his

nose into her shoulder, "does that answer your question?"

"I suppose so." She drew away a little.

He sat up. "All right, what's the problem?" he asked peevishly. "We're here, you wanted to come up here, but we're stuck talking about Tina and her bedmates. Let's get it out of the way, shall we?"

"All right. I just want to believe that you weren't so jealous of Tina's other lovers that you didn't—"

"Kill her?" He laughed. "There's something I should have told you. I *couldn't* have killed Tina. You know why? Because all day Saturday and Sunday, I was at Corsair's sales conference. Tina was supposed to go to the conference on Sunday, after she'd received that stupid award. Anyway, hundreds of people saw me at the conference and can vouch for every minute of my time. I was never alone—and even if I had been, I couldn't have slipped away to Shady Hills, New Jersey, because the conference was held at the Rye Town Hilton in Rye Brook, New York—fifty miles away!"

That was that, then. He snuggled back down into her shoulder. "You smell so nice," he said. She was overcome by a feeling of revulsion. She had to get out of there.

"Wait!" she cried.

He pulled back. "Wait?"

"Lock the door," she growled, curling her upper lip.

"Right! You got it." He ran over to the door, locked it, and hurried back. "Now, where were we?"

"I think we were about to make ourselves more comfortable."

"Ah! Of course." He squirmed out of his jacket and

threw it on the floor, yanked off his tie, and began unbuttoning his shirt, revealing a hairless flabby chest and a soft little belly.

"What about you?" he said, eyebrows wiggling.

"You first—I'm having too much fun watching."

"You got it." He pulled off his shirt, threw it onto the pile, and kicked off his shoes. Then he unfastened his belt, unzipped his fly, and kicked off his trousers to reveal green silk boxer shorts.

"Keep going!" she panted in a husky voice.

"Yes!" he cried, and off came the boxers.

Not much there, she thought, but she smiled lustily as she got up from the sofa.

"My turn," she said. "Now close your eyes."

He giggled. "Okay." He shut his eyes tight.

When she was certain he wasn't peeking, she snatched up all his clothes, ran to the door, and burst out of his office, zooming past Adele's desk.

"Jane! Come back!" she heard him cry as she punched repeatedly at the elevator button. Immediately one of the doors slid open.

"Adele!" she heard him shout. "Don't—"

There was a very long, high-pitched scream, so loud that she heard it even as the elevator descended to the lobby. Nearly doubled over with laughter, Jane got off the elevator and approached the guard at the reception desk.

"Do me a favor," she said, dumping Rafe's clothes on the desk. "Bring these up to Mr. Parker. I think he needs them."

Still laughing, she went out to the street, thrust her arm into the air, and hollered, "Taxi!"

Chapter Fourteen

In the taxi her cell phone rang. It was Daniel. "Jane, you got a call from a Shelly Adams. She wants you to call her. Here's her number. Ready?" She wrote it down. "Oh—and there was a strange call, believe it or not, from Rafe Parker. He said to give you a message."

She smiled. "Yes?"

"He said, 'Very funny!'" Daniel sounded puzzled. "Weren't you going to see him today?"

"That's right."

"So did you see him?"

"Yeah, more than I cared to!"

"Excuse me?"

"Never mind. Thanks, my friend. I'll see you later."

She dialed Shelly Adams's number.

"Jane," Shelly said, "can we talk again? There's something I've decided to tell you. It's about Tina."

"All right, sure. Give me your address."

Jane wrote it down. "I'll be there in a few min-

utes." Closing her phone, she told the driver to
take her to Shelly's address on the Lower East Side
instead of to the Port Authority.

"It's your money, lady," the driver said, and
changed course.

Shelly lived on Henry Street on the Lower East
Side. The doorway to her apartment building was
wedged between a Kosher delicatessen and a soup
kitchen called God's Harvest. A foot from the heavily scratched green door stood a garbage can from
which emanated a stench that made Jane recoil. It
had no lid and with a grimace she peeked in and
then was sorry she had: At the bottom lay a dead
rat, halfway through the process of decomposi-
tion, crawling with maggots.

She jumped away and hurried through the door
into a tiny airless vestibule. Inside on the left was a
buzzer board, one of its buttons labeled *Adams*. She
pressed it. Immediately the door was buzzed open
and she went through.

"Hi—up here!"

Jane looked straight up to the second-floor land-
ing. Shelly stood waving and smiling. "Come on
up."

Shelly was waiting by an open door to one of the
apartments on the second floor. "Hi, thanks for
coming," she said, and opened the door all the
way to reveal a studio apartment that was closer to
being just a room. Against the right wall stood a
stove, sink, and mini-refrigerator. A few feet away
from this "kitchen" was an open door to a bathroom. Straight ahead sat a battered leather sofa—a
pullout sofa bed, Jane surmised, since there was no
bed in sight—with an old trunk serving as a coffee
table in front of it. Behind the sofa and on the

right wall were exceptionally large windows, open to the hot July air.

"Come in, come in." Shelly closed the door behind Jane. She looked very different from how she had looked at the Windmere. No more prim skirt and blouse: Today she wore miniscule white shorts and an acid yellow halter top. She was barefoot and her hair was piled onto her head in a messy tangle.

She must have noticed Jane looking at her, because she said, "Forgive the outfit. No need to dress up for work anymore, right?" She smiled brightly.

"Right," Jane said. "How have you been?"

"Just so-so. As bad as Tina could be, I miss having a job, being part of things. She really was quite an important person. She knew practically everybody. It was exciting taking phone calls from Bill Clinton ... Gloria Vanderbilt ... Tama Janowitz. Now I feel so—out of it, so unimportant."

Jane sat down on the sofa. "You're not unimportant," she said, feeling as if she were talking to a daughter. "We're all important. And talking to those people didn't make you any more important than you are."

"I know; you're right. But you get what I mean. It's hard not being in the swim of things anymore. I don't know what to do with myself."

"Well, you can get a new job, for starters."

"Of course I'm trying to do that. I applied for several immediately. Nothing's come through yet, though. It is a difficult job market."

"True."

They sat silently for a moment, an awkward tension between them.

Shelly's eyes brightened. "Can I get you some

coffee? A cold drink? Actually," she said with an embarrassed smile, "that would be instant coffee or water with maybe an ice cube if I can pry one out of the tray."

"No, thank you, Shelly, I'm fine. Now, what was it you wanted to tell me about Tina?"

Shelly sighed deeply, her thin shoulders rising and dropping. "Yes, right. I wanted to tell you what Ian meant when he told you there was more to me than met the eye. By the way," she added quickly, "don't worry about Nat coming in. I've sent him to the grocery store with a long list."

Jane nodded, waiting.

Shelly said, "I suppose I should just tell you." She looked Jane square in the eye, her expression almost defiant. "Tina Vale . . . was my mother."

Jane blinked. "Your what?"

Shelly nodded simply. "Mm-hm. My mother. Mommy Dearest." She giggled self-consciously.

Was that why Shelly looked so familiar? Jane wondered. She sputtered, unsure what to say. "But—but—why was it a secret? Or was it?"

"Oh yes, absolutely. Ian knows, of course, but no one else." Shelly's face grew sad. "My father is an Italian businessman my mother met on a vacation in Sicily."

"Do you have a relationship with him? Do you see him?"

"Oh, no! He and I have never met. Mother would never allow it. I don't even know his name; I've never seen a picture of him, never spoken to him. I'm not even sure if he's still alive . . . or if he really existed at all."

"What do you mean?"

Shelly shrugged. "It's very romantic, you know, saying that my father is an Italian businessman. Very *Summertime*—you know, that movie with Katharine Hepburn? Sometimes I think that's where Mother got the idea—though it could be true. I don't know. Or my father could be any one of the zillions of men my mother has slept with over the years. Maybe she didn't even know which one of them was my father!"

"Where did your last name come from?"

"Adams? Oh, that's just a name Mother came up with to keep the truth a secret. It could just as easily have been Smith or Jones or Miller. I've never lived with Tina. I was raised by a distant cousin of hers in Grand Rapids. Four years after I graduated college, I asked Mother if I could come out to New York. To my amazement, she said yes—that in fact I could be her assistant. But no one must ever know I was her daughter. I would keep my phony last name, have my own place to live—she rented me this place—and never tell a soul."

"It must have been strange to work for your mother."

"It wasn't strange; it was wonderful." Shelly's gaze searched Jane's face. "It's probably hard for you to understand, because I know you must have hated my mother the way everyone else did—and with good reason. But she was still my mother. In all my years growing up in Michigan I saw her twice, once when I was five and once when I was thirteen. I thought she was the most beautiful, glamorous, exciting creature I'd ever seen. She brought me presents, told me about New York City, kissed me on the cheek . . . and then went away again. When she went away those two times—those were the worst moments of my life. When I asked her if I could come to New York and she not only said yes but offered me a job at Bleecker Books as her secretary, I couldn't believe my ears. It was literally a dream come true. When she got the job at Corsair, she took me with her."

Jane frowned, puzzled. "But if you so loved being with her, why did you quit your job on Saturday?"

Shelly laughed, waving her hand dismissively. "Oh, that wasn't the first time I'd quit. I'd done it twice before. She was always so mean to me. Sometimes I just couldn't take it. Saturday was the first time I quit because of how mean she was being to someone else—you. I fully intended to go back . . . and she would have taken me. But now I can't go back. I've got to find a real job, or else move back to Grand Rapids, and I'd rather die than do that."

Jane said, "I can't imagine what it must have been like to be her daughter."

"No, you can't. It was quite awful nearly all the time. She didn't really know me, yet I had to constantly hear over the telephone that I wasn't ambitious enough, or smart enough, or pretty enough for Mother, who had been all of those things. It was especially horrifying to her that I didn't go to a 'good' college."

Gently, Jane put a hand on the young woman's knee. "You've had a rough time. I hope you'll never let those things your mother said become part of you. Because you *are* important, and you *are* a good person."

"Thank you, Jane." Shelly's gaze dropped, tears in her eyes.

"Tell me," Jane said. "What made you decide to tell me this?"

The young woman shook her head, frowning. "I'd never met you until Saturday—though I'd spoken to you on the telephone, of course. But when I met you, I felt an instant connection. I can't explain it. I . . . wanted you to be my friend. I wanted you to know this about me. I think it was because of this strange connection I felt with you that I needed to come tell you how badly I felt about the way Mother treated you. Lord knows Mother treated a lot of people badly, yet I'd never felt compelled to tell them I was sorry."

Giving Shelly's knee another gentle pat, Jane rose. "Thank you. It means a lot that you've confided in me this way. I promise to keep your secret. And yes," she added with a warm smile, "we will be friends."

A tear rolled down Shelly's cheek and she wiped it away. She sniffed. "Well, I guess that's enough excitement for one afternoon, huh?"

Jane laughed. "I guess so!" she said, and an image of Rafe Parker sitting naked except for his black dress socks flashed into her mind. "I think I've had just about as much excitement as I can take for one day."

At the apartment door, the two women embraced briefly. "I'll keep your phone number," Jane said, "and I'll call you. We can have lunch."

"I'd love that."

"Good." With a decisive nod, Jane went out the door and down the stairs to the street.

* * *

When she got back to the office there was a message from Rafe Parker to call him.

"I hope you're proud of yourself."

"Sure am." She giggled.

"Adele quit. She's been with me for twelve years."

"My condolences. I'd have thought she was used to your antics."

"Not seeing me naked!"

"You did have your socks on."

"Mm," he grumbled, and paused. "I suppose you're going to try to extort a bigger offer out of me to keep quiet about what happened."

She laughed. "I wouldn't dream of telling anyone. Besides which, I don't work that way, Rafe. People like you and Tina may, but I don't."

"Mm," came another grumble. "Have you talked to Goddess?"

"Not yet."

"Why the hell not?" he hollered.

"Because I've been busy!" she hollered back.

"Get back to me."

"Of course I will," she said, and suddenly an idea occurred to her. "Rafe, there is something I need you to do for me."

"I thought you didn't work that way."

"I said I wouldn't extort a bigger offer for Goddess out of you, but there is something else I want."

"And what is that?"

"The rights back to the last book on Salomé Sutton's contract. We'll repay the advance she's received."

"I thought she was repped by Jory Mankewitz."

"She was. She's my client now."

"Good luck. Woman's a brute."

"Well?"

"Yeah, sure—who cares!"

"Have your contracts department draw up the papers—now."

"Fine." He hung up.

Jane jumped up from her desk. "Yes!"

Feeling energized, she called Goddess's townhouse in New York City and was lucky enough to find her at home.

"Hey, babe, how're they hangin'?"

"Fine, thanks. Yours?"

"So-so. I'm getting a little tired of the show, you know? Need somethin' fresh."

"But aren't you making that movie, *Taking It?*"

"Yeah," Goddess replied boredly, "but I need something *now.*"

"I've got just the thing. Another book."

"Another book! That first book nearly killed me."

"Uh, excuse me, Goddess, but you didn't write it."

"So? I had to read it, didn't I? That's a lot of work."

"I guess it is," she agreed thoughtfully. "Anyway, today I had an interesting lunch with Rafe Parker, chairman of the board of Corsair Publishing. He wants a sequel. He's made you an offer. Seven-point-five million."

"Oh yeah?" Goddess was barely fazed. "Interesting. What would it be about?"

"You, of course. A continuation of the last book."

"But the last book only came out last month.

You want me to write about my life for the past month?"

"No, of course not. You could pick another theme. Your views on various subjects. Or tell us about experiences you never mentioned in the first book."

"Hey!" Goddess said. "I could tell the whole story about my sister, and the murder . . ."

Jane shifted uneasily in her chair. "No, I don't think that would be a good idea. Why don't you give it some thought and get back to me. I think it really would be quite good for your career."

"Would I have to work with that whiny woman again?"

"Carmela Gold?"

"Yeah."

"Not if you don't want to. I can get you anyone you like. Or I could present you with a number of candidates."

"I like that last idea. Let me think it over, talk to Yves," Goddess said, referring to her manager.

"Very good," Jane said, and they rang off.

"You're a miracle worker!" Salomé Sutton boomed. "I mean, we're talkin' Helen Keller here."

"I'm glad you're as pleased as I am, Sal. So now you'll sign my full representation agreement, right? Become a full-fledged client?"

"Absolutely. Send it to me and I'll sign it. Now we gotta plan our strategy—you know, for where we're gonna sell the book now."

"Right. I'll give it some thought and call you again."

"Beautiful. Thanks, babe."

Jane hung up grinning. In several ways, this had been a very good day.

That night, just after nine, Daniel called.

"A stroke of luck, Jane. When I called Stein's office, the secretary gave me the last appointment *today*, though of course I never showed up. The appointment was for four-thirty. I watched the building from Fifth Avenue, just the way you said."

"Where are you now?

"I'm in the Village, but I'll tell you about that in a minute."

"Okay. Go on."

"Stein came out of the building around ten after five. I guess they waited for me until five and gave up. Anyway, he walked to Fifth Avenue and got in a cab. Fortunately there are lots of cabs going down Fifth at that time of day. I grabbed the next one and said, 'Follow that cab!' Can you believe I actually said that?"

"See, I knew you'd enjoy this spying thing. Then what happened?"

"We followed him all the way down to the Village. He got out in front of a bar called The Lure on West Thirteenth Street, and I got out and followed him inside."

"What was it like?"

"Different from anyplace I've ever been, that's for sure. Lots of leather, Levis, and uniforms."

"A gay bar, you're trying to say."

"Uh, yes."

"And? What did he do?"

"I lost him for a minute. All these half-naked guys started coming on to me."

"Can you blame them?"

He ignored this. "But I found him again. He was sitting at the bar, alone, having a drink. Then he went to watch one of these little shows that were going on in the front room. In the one he was watching, a guy was wrapping up another guy in Saran Wrap."

"Mm, to keep him fresh, no doubt."

"No doubt. Anyway, here's the important part. While Stein was watching the show, a good-looking young guy with black hair came up behind him and put his hands over Stein's eyes. Stein turned around and they kissed on the lips . . . a *long* kiss on the lips. After that I figured I'd gotten my answer and left."

"Yes, you'd definitely gotten your answer. Thanks, Double-O-Seven, you've done an admirable job. You may return to headquarters."

"Thanks, J. See you tomorrow."

Later, as Jane prepared for bed, Stanley called. "No prints on the toaster in your car."

"Did you really think there would be? There weren't any on the toaster in Tina's tub, either, right?"

"No."

"Well, thanks for letting me know."

"Sure. Jane?"

"Yes?"

"Please be careful."

She smiled. "I will, Stanley, I promise. Good night."

Lying in bed, she chuckled at the thought of Daniel at The Lure. But these thoughts quickly passed, and even as she waited for sleep she found herself recounting over and over again the amazing thing Shelly Adams had told her.

It occurred to Jane that Shelly's revelation put a whole new spin on things. Being Tina's daughter meant that Shelly knew more about her mother's life than she would have if she had been simply her secretary. Did this knowledge put Shelly in danger? Lying in bed, Winky and Twinky curled tightly together at the edge of her pillow, she stared at the ceiling, unable to sleep.

But eventually sleep did come, and it was in her sleep, when important things often occurred to Jane, that she had a realization so deeply disturbing that it jolted her awake. She had sat up suddenly in her bed, and Winky and Twinky stood watching her. She glanced at her bedside clock. It was only 2:30.

She got out of bed, showered, dressed, went downstairs and made strong coffee. She went to her study off the living room and tried to read a manuscript she had brought home from the office, but no matter how many times she read the same paragraphs, they meant nothing, as if they were written in a language she didn't know.

The hours couldn't pass quickly enough. Finally, after Nick and Florence had awakened and breakfasted, and Jane had driven Nick down the hill to middle school, she pulled over to the side of the road and called Shelly Adams on her cell phone.

"Hi, Jane! Listen, it was so great to see you yesterday. Thank you again for all the wonderful things you said. For being so supportive."

"Shelly," Jane said, not listening, "is Nat there?"

"No, he went out early. Said he had to do some more research at the New York Public Library for his new novel. He'll be out all day."

"Shelly, I need to see you again."

"Is something wrong?"

"I'll explain everything when I get there. I'll drive into the city. It's rush hour. With any luck I'll be there in an hour and a half."

"Okay," Shelly said, sounding baffled. "I'll see you then."

Fortunately, traffic was no worse than usual, and Jane made it to the Lower East Side in a little over an hour. She found a parking spot right on Henry Street, only a few doors down from Shelly's building.

In the stuffy vestibule, she buzzed Shelly's apartment and waited. There was no answer. Frowning, she tried the door; it was locked. Perhaps Shelly was in the bathroom, maybe showering. Jane waited a few more minutes and buzzed again. Still no answer. She hated doing this, but she pressed the four other buzzers. From the speaker came a man's raspy voice: "Who is it?"

She didn't know what to say. "You don't know me," she began, feeling like a fool, "but I'm a friend of Shelly Adams in apartment 2B. She's not answering her buzzer and I'm afraid something's wrong."

There was a brief silence; then, "Get the hell out of here before I call the police."

With a discouraged sigh Jane rattled the door, but even as old and decrepit as it was, it held fast. She heard a sound outside the door of the building and turned to see a young man coming in. He looked at her and smiled. Quickly Jane spun around and shouted into the intercom, "Okay, I'll be right up!"

The young man opened the door with his key and held it for Jane. "Thanks," she said, and ran up the stairs. At the door to Shelly's apartment she waited a few moments, until the young man had passed this floor and continued up the stairs. Turning back to Shelly's door, Jane raised her hand to knock, then noticed that the door was ajar. She pushed it open a little more.

"Shelly?"

There was no answer.

Her heart beginning to thump, she took hold of the knob, entered the apartment, and gasped.

Chapter Fifteen

Shelly's apartment looked as if a giant had picked up the room and shaken it, very hard. A small bookcase Jane hadn't noticed on her visit the day before lay on its side, books strewn across the floor. A drying rack had been knocked off the counter next to the sink and lay on the floor, knives and forks and spoons lying amid shards of broken dishes. The trunk that served as a coffee table sat at a right angle to the sofa now. And on the sofa itself were strange dark marks Jane couldn't identify. Walking over to it, she drew in her breath and put her hand to her mouth.

It was blood. A lot of it. Smeared across the seat and back cushions, big dark congealing puddles and smudges that trailed away as if made by a paint brush without enough paint.

"Oh dear Lord," she whispered, looking around, then rushed to the bathroom to look inside. Nothing appeared out of place.

Emerging from the bathroom, she noticed the

bookcase again and saw a framed photograph lying amid the books. She picked it up. It was a picture of Shelly and Tina, taken recently. It was a close-up and they were smiling. Studying Shelly's face, Jane nodded.

She was right—she was sure of it now.

Crying, she ran from the apartment, down the stairs, and out to the street, where people passed with obscene indifference. She started to take her cell phone from her purse, then realized she mustn't use it. Up at the corner of Clinton Street she spotted a pay phone. She ran toward it, passing her car, and picked up the receiver. The phone was dead, like many other pay phones in New York. Glancing around, she spotted another one at the opposite corner and ran through traffic to it. It worked. She dialed 911.

"Something terrible has happened," she told the officer who answered.

"Tell me your name, please, and where you are?"

She gave the woman Shelly's address. "Apartment 2B. Hurry. There's blood, a lot of blood."

"Ma'am," the officer said calmly, "is the person—"

Jane hung up, looking about quickly before running back across the intersection and down Henry Street to her car. Half a minute later, as she turned off Clinton Street to go up East Broadway, the wail of a police siren pierced the air.

She had to see Stanley. He was the only one she could talk to right now, the only one in whom she could confide her realization.

It took an hour to reach Shady Hills. She drove

directly to the police station and nearly collided with him as she entered the low glass-and-brick building.

"Whoa!" he laughed, holding her by the upper arms.

"Oh, Stanley," she said, putting her arms around him, and began to cry.

"Jane, what's wrong? What's going on?"

He escorted her inside to his small cinder-block office and closed the door. "Now, can you tell me why you're so upset?"

She looked up, tears running down her face, and sniffed. She took some tissues from her bag and wiped her eyes and nose. She laughed a little. "I must be a sight."

"No, you're as beautiful as always. Now, are you going to tell me what's wrong or not?"

"I don't know where to start."

"Start anywhere."

"All right. Shelly Adams, the young woman—"

"Tina Vale's secretary. Yes?"

"She's Tina's daughter."

"Her *daughter?*"

"Yes. Shelly told me so herself yesterday. But there's more, something Shelly didn't tell me because she doesn't know. Do you remember I said that Tina told me she and Kenneth had had an affair?" He nodded. "Well . . ." She took a deep breath. "Kenneth was Shelly's father."

His jaw dropped and his eyes bulged. "*Your* Kenneth?"

"Yes, my Kenneth. It all came together last night—I couldn't sleep. Shelly had said Tina always told her that her father was an Italian businessman Tina had met on a vacation in Sicily. But

Tina had never told Shelly anything about him, never showed her his photograph, never allowed her to see him, never even told her his name. That was because Tina didn't want anyone to know—not even Shelly herself—that she had borne Kenneth's child."

"But how can you be sure?"

"Because I've seen it all along. The first time I met Shelly she looked familiar to me, but I couldn't figure out why. When I found out Shelly was Tina's daughter, I thought *that* was why—I was seeing Tina in her. But that wasn't it. Shelly didn't even look like Tina. The person I was seeing was Kenneth."

He considered all this. At last he said, "But wouldn't Kenneth have told you?"

She shook her head helplessly. "How do we know Kenneth was even aware of it?"

"I'd bet anything he was. You've told me Tina hated you because Kenneth left her for you. Tina wanted Kenneth desperately. Wouldn't she have used the baby as a means of getting Kenneth back?"

"Yes, you're right," she said thoughtfully. "I'm sure she would have. But he didn't go to her."

"No, Jane," he said kindly, "he didn't go to her. He stayed with you, the woman he loved."

"But to know all those years and not tell me! Shelly told me she'd never met her father, but do you think Kenneth ever saw her? He would have had to know Tina had sent her to Grand Rapids, but if he had known he might have gone out there. Watched her from afar, that kind of thing."

He pondered this. "If he knew where she was, he probably went to see her. I would. I think most

men would. Would he have helped Tina financially?"

"Maybe," Jane said, "but I doubt it. She always
made a lot of money, probably as much as if not
more than he did. And she was extremely proud. I
doubt she'd have taken it even if he'd offered."

"Well, you'll never know, Jane. You're not thinking of starting up some kind of relationship with
this girl because she's Kenneth's daughter, are
you?"

The tears came again, popping from her eyes. "I
can't!" she said, wiping her eyes with her hands.
"She's dead!"

"What?"

She nodded quickly. "I called her early this morning. After I realized she was Kenneth's daughter, I
had to see her again. I wasn't going to tell her. I
don't know what excuse I was going to make for
appearing the next day, but I'd figure something
out. The important thing was to see her again
knowing what I knew. I called her this morning,
right after I dropped Nick off at school. But when
I got there"—she felt the tears coming again but
fought them back—"the door was open. The apartment was a wreck, as if there had been a terrible
struggle. And, Stanley, there was blood—a lot of
blood—all over the sofa. She's dead, I'm sure of
it."

He sat up straight in his chair. "Did you call the
police?"

"Yes, from a pay phone, but I didn't tell them who
I was."

He gave a short, rueful laugh. "Good. Being a
suspect in one murder is enough."

"Stanley, this isn't funny! Someone has killed

this poor girl and taken her body somewhere, and it's the same person who killed Tina, the same lunatic who killed that poor creature and left it in my car. Shelly knew more than she let on, much more. And it got her killed."

"Apparently so," he agreed quietly. "I've got a couple of friends at NYPD. I'll see what I can find out, what they're thinking."

"All right," she said, rising. "Thank you, Stanley."

He put his arm around her and walked her to her car. "I think you should go home and get some rest. You said yourself you barely got any sleep last night."

She shook her head. "It wouldn't do any good. I'm too riled up. I'll go to the office, try to take my mind off this. But you have to promise to tell me if you hear anything."

"I promise," he said.

In her rearview mirror she saw him waving to her, his face troubled, as she pulled out of the police station's parking lot.

She didn't go straight to the office. Instead of continuing on Packer Road to the village green, she took a right onto Highland, then left onto Cranmore Avenue, passing the Senior Center, where Doris volunteered, on the right.

Very soon she reached a sign that said SHADY HILLS CEMETERY and pulled the car to the side of the quiet, sun-dappled road. A black wrought-iron fence ran along the front of the cemetery, in its center a gate through which Jane passed, ascending a paved path that wound gently through well-tended grass dotted with gravestones in perfect rows. At the very top of the hill she left the path, walking across the grass to stand in front of one of the graves.

KENNETH ADAM STUART
BELOVED HUSBAND AND FATHER

"Hello, Kenneth," she said, smiling. "I'm sorry I haven't been here in a while, but I think of you a lot; you know I do."

From the woods bordering the back of the cemetery came that odd soft-screeching chatter of a flock of starlings, like the patter of a summer rainstorm; then suddenly they rose together into the air, a black cloud against the hot blue sky.

She looked down again at Kenneth's grave, scratching her head and then shaking back her hair, unsure how to begin.

"Kenneth," she said at last, "I came to tell you that I know. I know about you and Tina, that you were with her before you met me, and then again while we were all working together at Silver and Payne. It's okay, because you left her for me, Kenneth darling, but *why* didn't you tell me about the baby? You did know about it; I'm sure you did. Tina must have told you she was pregnant, must have tried to use the baby to get you back.

"What I don't understand is why you never told *me*. Didn't you trust me? Did you think I wouldn't understand? That I would leave you?" Tears streamed down Jane's cheeks. "I wouldn't have, you know, darling. I swear I wouldn't. Why? Why didn't you tell me?"

And then the oddest feeling came over her. She

felt overcome by a wave of warm comfort, as if Kenneth himself were taking her face in his strong hands as he used to do.

And all at once she knew the answer. It was the same answer Stanley had given her Saturday morning.

He didn't tell her because he didn't want to hurt her. He loved her too much to tell her. She smiled. "Oh, Kenneth . . . I understand. Thank you."

She watched an ant make its way around the base of the gravestone, carefully circumventing each blade of grass.

"Did you ever see your daughter? She grew up to be very pretty. She looks so much like you. She's got your strong straight nose, your pale green eyes, your perfectly shaped mouth." She laughed. "Her hair is dark, probably Tina's natural color. Speaking of which, did you know Tina is married to a plastic surgeon? Who knows what's real anymore?

"But maybe you know what your daughter looks like—looked like. I don't know if you do, because Tina sent her away—far away, to Grand Rapids, Michigan, of all places. That's where your daughter grew up and became a fine young lady—you would have been proud, darling. And then she came out here to New York to work with her mother.

"That's when the trouble started. Because Tina's gone now. And Kenneth"—the tears increased, her face contorting—"I'm really sorry, but I also have to tell you that Shelly—that's your daughter's name, Shelly—is dead, too. I—I felt you should know. Maybe you already do. I'm not trying to hurt you; I just wanted you to know I'm doing all I can to find out what happened to her."

She took a handkerchief out of her purse and used it to wipe her eyes and nose. She laughed through her tears. "My mascara must be a mess! You always teased me about that, said I looked like a raccoon. I've tried those unsmudgeable mascaras but I don't like them, so—You don't want to hear about my makeup.

"I miss you, Kenneth. I'll always miss you. As I've told you, I'm seeing a lovely man. Stanley, Stanley Greenberg. He's with the Shady Hills Police Department, a detective. I know you'd like him. In fact, if you were still here, I'm sure the two of you would be fast friends.

"And Nicholas, he's doing so well. He's so tall you wouldn't believe it. He's eleven—in the sixth grade, middle school, can you believe it? He'd make you very proud. He's very handsome, looks so much like you, too.

"Well, Kenneth darling, I suppose I'd better go now, get back to work. The agency's doing very well, by the way. I'm making bigger deals and more money, so it's not a worry anymore, the way it used to be. Nick keeps asking if we can put in a swimming pool, and I just may do it! You always looked so handsome in your swimsuit. I remember how you used to show off for me with your fancy dives and silly belly flops. Well.

"Daniel's doing better and better, too. Someday—who knows?—maybe I'll make him my partner. I would like that."

She carefully folded her handkerchief and replaced it in her purse. "Good-bye, Kenneth. I miss you. And I love you. I always will."

Pulling her gaze from the gravestone, she turned and started down the hill. Then she abruptly stopped, turned, and walked back to Kenneth's grave. *Kenneth Adam Stuart.*

Shelly *Adams.*

Yes, it all made sense.

She couldn't go back to the office, not yet. She parked behind her building but walked through the alley between the buildings, crossed Center Street, and took one of the paths across the green. At the other side, she went into Whipped Cream, hoping Ginny would be there.

She was, pouring a cup of coffee for an elderly redheaded woman seated in front of the used-brick fireplace wall.

"Hey, babe," Ginny said, looking up, and immediately her face grew concerned. "What's the matter? Why have you been crying?"

Jane sat down at a table against the small café's opposite wall. "I haven't been. Who said anything was the matter? I'm just tired is all."

Ginny sighed in irritation, crossed the room to Jane's table, and sat down. "You better tell me fast, because any minute either George or Charlie is going to show up and holler at me for sitting down. They hate it when I do this."

Jane laughed. She knew that in truth, George and Charlie, the café's owners, were extremely fond of Ginny and treated her like family. Ginny had once said that if she ever left Whipped Cream, she didn't know what they would do.

"So what's up?" Ginny said.

"Oh, it's Nicholas. Giving me a hard time, as all eleven-year-olds give their mothers a hard time."

Ginny eyed her suspiciously. "A hard time about what?"

"Oh . . . school."

Ginny put her hand over Jane's. "Spill it, girl-friend."

Jane withdrew her hand. "What are you, some kind of mind reader?"

"No, just your best friend. And if you can't tell me what's bothering you, who are you gonna tell?"

"You're right," Jane said, putting her hand back on the table and patting Ginny's. "It's not a short story, though. What about George and Charlie?"

Ginny shrugged. "Don't worry about them."

So Jane told her—about Shelly's revelation that she was Tina's daughter, about Jane's realization that Kenneth was Shelly's father, and about returning to Shelly's apartment and finding evidence of her murder. She began to cry again.

"Oh, babe, that's horrible," Ginny said, and broke into tears of her own.

"Ginny!" came George's gravelly voice from behind the counter. They looked up and saw only the top of his head.

"I'm here, George."

"I *know* you're there. How about getting back to work?"

"Is there more?" Ginny asked Jane softly.

"No, that's about it. Isn't that enough?"

Ginny rose, taking up her coffeepot. "I'd say so. Coming, George!" To Jane she said, "So what are you going to do? About Shelly, I mean?"

"There's nothing I *can* do. I told the police."

Ginny nodded. "I'm sorry, hon. That's rough. Listen, if you need to talk some more, you call me, all right?"

"Will do," Jane promised.

The bell on the café door jangled softly and they looked up. It was Audrey Fairchild, who lived across the street from Jane. Pretty Audrey had her honey blond hair pulled back into its customary ponytail. Her face, as always, was perfectly made up, from her powder pink eye shadow to her brownish-plum lipstick. She wore a vibrant pink print Capri set and white sandals.

"Well, if it isn't Miss Sunshine," Ginny muttered under her breath.

Seeing Jane and Ginny, Audrey broke into an enormous smile. "Well hi, dolls! Janey, what are you doing here, you naughty girl? Shouldn't you be over at your office"—she made a mischievous face, her eyes opening wide—"or killing someone?"

The elderly red-haired woman glanced up in alarm.

"Audrey," Ginny said, "that's not funny."

"Ooh, sorry!" Audrey said, taking a seat in the middle of the room. "It's just that the whole town is buzzing, Jane. You, who always solve murders, are a suspect in one!"

Ginny handed her a menu.

"Don't need it," Audrey said. "Just bring me that chocolate creation you whipped up for me last week. I can't stop thinking about it. I must have it! I don't care how much weight I gain."

Jane and Ginny both rolled their eyes. Audrey had been a size 6 for as long as they had known her. No matter what she ate, she never put on an ounce, and for that, Jane and Ginny hated her.

"You mean the Mocha-Choca?" Ginny asked.

"That's it! Bring me one before I positively expire."

"You got it," Ginny said, and tossing Jane a conspiratorial smile, went behind the counter and began pouring ingredients into the blender.

"So what's up, Jane?" Audrey asked, crossing her shapely legs. "Read any good books lately?" She barked out a laugh.

Audrey always asked Jane that, and always seemed to think it was riotously funny. Jane had long ago stopped bothering to answer this question. She just smiled. "How are Elliott and Cara?"

Recently Audrey and her husband, Elliott, had gotten back together after a separation. Cara, their daughter, was a horrendously spoiled sixteen-year-old.

"Elliott's fine—working too hard, as usual." Elliott was medical director of the New Jersey Rehabilitation Institute in nearby West Orange. "As for Cara, I swear that girl is going to drive me to an early grave."

"Why?" Jane asked, though she hadn't the slightest interest. "What's she done?"

"You know she's just gotten her learner's permit, right?"

Jane didn't know, but she nodded.

"She's driving me nuts! One minute she wants a BMW, the next minute it's an Audi, the next minute it's a Lexus. I said, 'Cara, make up your mind!' "

"Mm," Ginny said dryly, appearing with Audrey's Mocha-Choca, "that is enough to drive a body mad."

Jane nearly burst out laughing. Ginny was so good for her. She rose. "Good-bye, ladies. Have a lovely afternoon."

Audrey made a pouty face. "Aren't you going to stay and chat?"

"Nope. This naughty girl's gotta get back to work." And feeling better than she had when she came in, she left Whipped Cream and headed back across the green to her office.

But she didn't take up her work when she got there; she sat staring at the heap, interested in none of it.

Daniel buzzed her. "Nat Barre on one."

She grabbed it. "Nat?"

"Jane? Have you heard from Shelly, by any chance? I can't find her?"

How could he be so calm? "Nat, are you at her apartment?"

"No, I'm at the library, researching. I've been calling and calling, and she doesn't answer. She told me about the nice chat you and she had, so I thought maybe you'd know where she is."

She wanted so badly to tell him what she'd discovered, but she couldn't, couldn't spare his seeing it for himself. Then it occurred to her that the police were no doubt already there. They'd keep him out. "I'm sorry, Nat, I . . . don't know."

"Okay," he said on a weary sigh. "If you do hear from her, let me know."

Feeling awful, she replaced the receiver and wandered out to the reception room, where she leaned against the credenza and brought Daniel up to date on everything, even telling him about Shelly's parentage.

"Unbelievable," he said, shaking his head. "I'm sorry, Jane. I mean, she was Nick's half-sister."

"Of course, you're right," she said. "I hadn't even thought of that." Sadness swept over her. "And he never knew her . . . and never will."

"So now what?" he said.

She shook her head. "There's something missing."

"What?"

"A missing piece. The key to everything."

Daniel shrugged. "Apparently it doesn't exist."

"No, that's not true. It always exists. You just have to know where to look for it."

"But you've looked everywhere."

She thought about this for a moment. Then she looked up and said, "Actually, I haven't."

He looked at her inquiringly.

"It's so obvious," she said. "Whose home have we not searched?"

"I give up."

"I'll give you a clue. It's the one place where the vital clue, the missing piece, is most likely to be."

All at once his face took on an expression of dread. "No."

"Yes. Tina Vale and Ian Stein's apartment, or condo, or house, or whatever it is."

"You can't."

"Of course I can. I have to. I have to get into their home and snoop around."

He looked aghast. "You can't, Jane! You'll get caught. You could be arrested. You . . ."

She wasn't listening to him. "But I'm afraid to do it alone. I'll need your help."

"Jane . . ."

"Oh, stop sounding like Ethel Mertz. We can do this—we've done harder things."

"Like what?"

She ignored him. "In fact," she said, a calculating look on her face, "I've already got a plan . . ."

Chapter Sixteen

Daniel squirmed on the car seat, pulling at his pant legs. "These coveralls are too tight in the crotch."

"Thanks for sharing," Jane said with a laugh. They emerged from the Lincoln Tunnel and she drove straight ahead, toward the Park & Lock on 42nd Street.

"Why are you going in here?"

"I don't want to have to worry about parking. Besides, I don't want my car seen."

Inside the parking garage, they found a spot and got out. Jane looked at Daniel and laughed. "I don't believe I've ever seen you dressed in anything even close to that. You look kind of hunky, actually."

He had borrowed a pair of gray cotton coveralls from a friend of Ginny's whose husband worked at a car wash in Boonton. Ignoring her remark, he wiggled around in the confining uniform.

"How do I look?" Jane asked him. "Convincing?"

Florence's friend Linda, who worked as a maid for a wealthy family at the north end of Shady Hills, had lent Jane one of her uniforms, a pale-blue short-sleeve cotton dress that buttoned up the front. She turned to face Daniel. "Does this look too big?"

He studied her. "No, just comfortably loose."

Linda was a size larger than Jane. "I should have worn a belt."

"Oh come on," he said impatiently. "Let's get this over with."

They left the garage and walked along 42nd Street to Tenth Avenue, where they hailed a cab that took them to Olympian House, the luxury high-rise on Central Park South in which Ian Stein now lived alone in a nine-room condominium.

Daniel handed the driver a few bills as a tip and they gazed up at the magnificent glass monolith. "How did you find out they lived here?" he asked Jane.

"It wasn't as hard as you might think. Believe it or not, I had help from Bertha."

"Bertha Stumpf?"

"Yup. Bertha may be a pain in the butt, but she's very well connected. For example, she's friends with Ellie Coburn."

"*The* Ellie Coburn?"

"The very one. Of Coburn and Clark Real Estate, which brokers many of the luxury condos in the city. Ellie knew right away where Tina and Ian lived."

"But how do we get inside?" he asked.

"Leave that to me." She looked him up and down approvingly. "Now remember, we have been sent by relatives of Dr. Stein."

She led the way in, past a bewildered doorman. The concierge came out from behind a massive semicircular desk of glass brick and eyed them disdainfully. "Service entrance in back. You should know that."

"I'm sorry," Jane said in a softly accented voice. "We don't usually work here. I was told you'd have a key to Dr. Stein's condo for us."

"Why would I have a key? Who are you?"

"We have been sent by Dr. Stein's aunt and uncle in California. They heard that the regular cleaning help quit when Ms. Vale passed away, and they sent us to fill in . . . as a gift, you know."

"A gift."

"That's right. Do you have the key?"

The concierge hesitated. "How do I know this is on the up and up?"

"Up and up?" Jane shook her head, looking puzzled. "I'm sorry, my English is not always so good. We should get started before the doctor comes home, or else we will not be finished and the gift will not work."

"A gift, eh?" The concierge was studying her, pondering. "Okay, I'll tell you what I'll do. I'll let you into Dr. Stein's place and check on you in half an hour. If I don't like the job you're doing, you're out."

Daniel looked alarmed. "Out? Why?"

The concierge looked at him suddenly, as if he were a tree that had just spoken. "Because," the concierge said belligerently, "this is Olympian House, and things gotta be done right. You don't do it right, you're outta here, gift or no gift. Seeing to things like that is *my* job."

"No problem, that's fine." Jane kept her tone subservient. "Thank you."

They followed him to one of the elevators hidden in an alcove around the corner from his desk; then the three of them rode silently together to the thirty-seventh floor. The elevator doors opened onto a corridor that reminded Jane of someone's living room, a softly lit space with dark pumpkin carpeting and upholstered walls to match. On a small side table of dark, deeply polished wood stood a foot-high pale-green jade sculpture of a hawk with its talons wrapped around a branch.

"Over here," the concierge said, walking to the right down the corridor to a door into which he inserted a key on a ring from his pocket. "Remember," he said, pushing the door open. "Half an hour." Suddenly he looked at them. "You know where the supplies are?"

"Yes," Jane said, smiling gratefully, "in the back, near the service entrance. We were told."

The man nodded and closed the door behind them, leaving them in complete darkness.

"Is there a switch?" Jane whispered.

"I don't feel one," Daniel said. "Wait, I think I see a lamp here." There was a click and a light came on, illuminating a vast foyer with a domed ceiling.

Jane let her gaze move around the condominium. "Oh my."

Beyond the foyer was the largest room Jane had ever seen, a vast expanse of pale hardwood floor that culminated in an entire wall of floor-to-ceiling glass. They walked slowly toward it, passing low, slinky Italian furniture and, on the walls, enormous sepia prints of seashells. Reaching the glass wall, they stared out at the roof of St. Patrick's Cathedral and, to the right, Fifth Avenue.

"Look at this," Daniel said, and Jane turned around.

At one end of the living room was a wide sweeping staircase with open treads that led up to a second floor. This floor had no wall separating it from the living room; it just ended in midair, as if held up magically.

"A person could get killed up there," Jane said.

"Yeah, get up at night for a glass of water and—bam!"

"Can you imagine kids in this house?" she said.

"No, and there never were any."

Jane thought about what Shelly had told her. "No," she agreed sadly, "there never were." She shook herself from her thoughts. "We'd better get to work. He'll be back in half an hour."

"Right. Now, what are we looking for?"

"*You're* not looking for anything. You're keeping watch at the door."

He looked disappointed. "All right." He walked back toward the foyer and stopped abruptly. "Hey, look at this."

He stood before a wall fitted from floor to ceiling with shelves of brushed gray metal. Spaced perfectly along these shelves were toasters, dozens and dozens of them, each different from the others, all antique. "This is cool."

"Never mind that," she snapped. "You've got to keep watch, remember? Hurry up."

Reluctantly he went to the door. "There's no peephole."

"Then open the door a crack and look out. If you see him coming, let me know."

He did as instructed, while she began her exploration. The living room yielded nothing of interest—aside from being the largest room she had ever seen. At the far left side of the room, Japanese-style sliding door, opened onto a dining room, beautiful for its highly polished, traditional furniture but without interest otherwise.

From here she explored the kitchen, which was at least three times the size of her own and contained ovens and sinks the likes of which Jane had never seen before. Had Tina ever actually cooked anything? Jane doubted it. There would be a housekeeper—dismissed, perhaps, since Tina's death.

In a corner of the kitchen was a sort of homemaker's desk, complete with state-of-the-art computer equipment. Jane decided not to get involved in turning on the computer and searching its files, a huge job in itself, but she did search the drawers of the hardwood desk and found only a telephone directory, a few pens, and a tattered paperback copy of Erica Jong's *Fear of Flying*. Jane leafed through the first few pages and found an inscription: *For Tina—Never be afraid to fly! Erica*. How odd, Jane thought, replacing the book in the drawer.

A long corridor extended from the kitchen. The first room opening off of it was a TV room, which contained a complete home theater system. There were a few drawers in the wall unit that contained this system, but they held only CDs, DVDs, and videocassettes.

Next along the hall was a library, equipped with floor-to-ceiling bookcases and two ladders on rollers. Jane gazed at it wistfully; she'd always wanted a room like this. She noted that one wall of the room was devoted entirely to books Tina had published during her years as an editor.

In the center of the room was a small antique desk. Its drawers opened easily and revealed only pads of paper and boxes of stationery—both Tina's and Ian's. But there were no letters, no notes, no scribbles on scraps of paper.

She moved on, examining a bathroom (only a bottle of aspirin in the medicine cabinet), a guest bedroom, and a home gym, but finding nothing of interest. Throughout Tina and Ian's home there was a sterile, impersonal quality, as if no one really lived there—no clutter, no mess, no quirky personal items. Like something out of *House Beautiful*, Jane thought, moving back down the corridor, through the kitchen to the living room, and up the sweeping staircase.

At the top of the stairs was an open sitting area from which could be seen the expanse of living room and the great glass wall looking over the city. Opening off the rear wall were three doors. One led to a study that was clearly Ian's. In the center of the room sat a glass-and-chrome desk without drawers. On the desk's surface were a computer and printer, a clock, a leather-framed photograph of the same dark-haired young man Ian Stein had shown Jane in his office, and a pad of white lined paper on which had been scribbled "Frank E. Campbell Funeral Chapel—81st & Madison." That was one funeral Jane would take a pass on.

Behind the desk sat a credenza, on top of which stood a row of medical books between bronze horse bookends. On the room's back wall was a window that looked out on the roofs of other buildings. The wall facing the desk was hung with an enormous Japanese screen depicting a plum tree in blossom against a gold background. "Magnificent," she murmured, gazing at it and thinking how well it would look above her mantel. Then she remembered the concierge and checked her watch. She had seven minutes left. She hurried out of Ian's study and through the next of the three doors.

This was clearly Ian's bedroom, a simple, masculine affair—bed and two night tables, dresser, armoire, a walk-in closet. The left night table drawer was empty. In the one on the right was a bottle of Listerine and a box of cough drops. She crossed quickly to the armoire and opened it. In its center were four tiny drawers containing cuff links, collar stays, and the like. Closing the armoire, she hurried to the closet but found only clothing, no drawers or compartments. A bathroom opened off Ian's bedroom. Jane threw open the medicine cabinet and found a row of over-the-counter items—Advil, NyQuil, Aleve, TheraFlu—and a half-empty prescription bottle of Valium. Jane laughed. She didn't wonder that Tina's husband needed Valium.

She hurried out and into the third room, Tina's room. It was filled with surprisingly feminine furniture—a canopy bed, a long, low dresser whose drawers contained neatly folded sweaters and jeans, an antique writing desk whose only drawer was empty. Didn't these people *do* anything besides work? Perhaps not.

Tina, too, had a walk-in closet. It was crammed messily with dresses and coats and furs and blouses and shoes. No drawers here, either.

Finally, Jane checked the bathroom, a vast chamber of white marble, complete with bidet, sauna, stall shower, and separate soaking tub. Once again she checked the medicine cabinet.

She frowned. Here were a surprising number of prescription bottles. The first one on the left was Paxil, which Jane knew was an antidepressant. Remembering what Shelly had said about Tina's seeing a therapist, Jane decided to write this down on a small pad she took from the pocket of her dress. She wondered what Tina Vale had had to be depressed about; she got everything she wanted (well, almost everything), and lived in a palace in the sky.

Beside the Paxil was a bottle of something called Rilutek. Jane copied this down, and did the same with the next two bottles: Lioresal and Zanaflex, neither of which she had ever heard of. There was an array of vitamins, along with bottles of Tylenol, Advil, then a prescription bottle of Ultram, which Jane had heard of—a painkiller.

"Jane!" Daniel called up to her in a urgent whisper. "He's coming!"

"Whoops," she said, closing the cabinet, and hurried out and down the stairs. Daniel waited at the bottom. "This way," she told him, and ran into the kitchen.

"Where are we going?" he asked.

"There's a service door in here—I noticed it before." It was at the back left corner of the room, at the side of a pantry. Jane unlocked it, pushed Daniel through, and then slid through herself, closing it just as the concierge's voice rang through the apartment.

"Hello? You here?"

Jane's heart was pounding. They were standing in a small, plain hallway, a far cry from the luxurious corridor by which they had entered the apartment. At the end of this corridor was a service elevator. Jane pressed the button.

"Nothing's happening," Daniel said nervously.

"Give it a chance!" she said, and after a moment the light in the button went out and the door slid slowly open.

Daniel put out his hand to press "L," but Jane stopped him. "No—press 'B.' Basement."

"Why?"

"Because he'll be looking for us in the lobby. I'm sure there's a way out through the basement."

"How are you so sure?"

"Just do it!"

He obeyed, and the elevator descended to the bottom of the building.

The doors opened onto absolute darkness.

"Great," Daniel grumbled. "Now what do we do?"

"We get out," Jane said, and pulled him into the blackness. The elevator door slid shut and they were alone in the dark.

"I can't even see my hands in front of my face," he said.

"Haven't you ever seen your hands before?"

"Funny. Really, Jane, how are we going to get out of here?"

"Sh-h-h! We look for light. I'm going to start moving slowly. Hold my hand so we don't get separated."

"I can't believe this," he said, allowing himself to be dragged along.

"Daniel," she whined, "quiet!"

"Okay, sorry!"

She hit a concrete post. "Ow! All right, we move

around the post. A few steps, hands out . . . what on earth?"

She had encountered something soft and pliable—fabric of some sort, that was it—and it was warm. "What the dickens . . . ?"

She moved her hands carefully up this strange object, felt metal buttons, then soft, warm flesh. She screamed. Daniel screamed.

Suddenly the basement was flooded with light and the concierge stood inches before them, an amused smirk on his face. "You two having fun?"

Jane put her hand to her chest. "I think I just had a heart attack."

"What are you doing down here?"

"We pressed the wrong button," Jane said, the accent back. "So sorry."

"Done upstairs already?"

"No," Daniel said, "we needed more supplies."

"Oh really? Like what?"

"Uh . . . Windex."

"Windex?"

"Yes. And Mop & Glo."

The concierge frowned. "Mop & Glo?"

"Yes," Jane said, "it's the only thing we use. Dr. Stein is all out."

He eyed her suspiciously and arched an eyebrow. "I looked around in there. Didn't look like you did much of anything."

She looked mightily affronted. "Not much of anything! We dusted, vacuumed—"

"Okay, okay." None too gently, he took them by the arms and walked them toward a door. "I'm sure the good doctor will enjoy his gift."

"But we're not finished!" Jane said, though she had no intention of coming back.

"Yes, you are. No Windex, no Mop & Glo. That's it." He opened the door, beyond which were concrete stairs up to the street level. "Have a nice day!" And he slammed the door behind them.

"Jerk," Jane said as they climbed the stairs. "Not letting us finish."

Daniel glared at her. "We weren't really cleaning!"

"*He* didn't know that. Come on, let's get a cab."

Chapter Seventeen

"Hand me my cell, would you please?" Jane turned the car off Route 495 onto Route 3. "I want to check the messages at the office."

There were two messages, the first one from Bertha Stumpf.

"Jane," came her whining voice, "hello, darling. Did you get the cover for *Shady Lady*? Well, I did, and it's a definite no-go. What were they thinking? Call me."

The second was from Nat Barre.

"Hi, Jane, it's Nat, Nat Barre. Could you call me, please, as soon as you can? Something's happened, something bad, and I need to talk to you. You remember I'm staying at Shelly's apartment." And he left the number.

With a heavy feeling in the pit of her stomach, she called Shelly's number. Nat answered on the first ring.

"Jane, it's horrible. I was out all day yesterday at the library, researching my new book. When I got back around five I found the apartment door open, the apartment in shambles, and blood all over the sofa. The police were already there."

"What did they say?"

"Some woman had called them. Who could it have been?"

"Maybe someone else in your building who saw something, was trying to help, but wanted to stay anonymous?"

"I don't know, Jane. I think this has to do with Tina Vale's murder. I think Shelly knew who killed Tina, and whoever that was killed Shelly."

"Let's not panic yet, Nat," she said, though she agreed with him about Shelly's fate. "Call the police, see if they've found out anything. Call me if you find out anything new, okay?"

"Okay," he said doubtfully, and hung up.

She had told Daniel about what she'd found at Shelly's apartment, and told him now what Nat had said. Daniel shook his head. "But if she's dead, where is her body?"

Jane shook her head. "No idea. Whoever killed her didn't want her body there. But why?"

For the rest of the day, she felt as if she were sleepwalking through her work. She gazed at contracts without seeing them, read manuscripts without comprehending them, wrote letters without knowing what she was writing. She made no phone calls; she was certainly in no mood for Bertha Stumpf and her whining today.

She left promptly at five. Driving through the village's golden streets, she realized it was unlikely that Tina Vale's real killer would be apprehended.

She remembered the issue of the *Post* that Ernie had held up for the ladies at the Defarge Club meeting. When the media got word that Jane was among the suspects, she would be ruined. She marveled that they didn't know it yet. As she pulled into her driveway a deep depression hit her, along with a pounding tension headache.

She sat in the family room with Nick, who was trying to teach Twinky some tricks.

"Jump, Twink!" he cried, dangling a kitty treat on a thread tied to his fishing rod. The tiny mottled cat leaped for the treat, fell back to the floor, and leaped again.

"What do you think of that, Mom? She's doing a trick!"

Jane gave him a wan smile and nodded, but Florence appeared in the doorway to the kitchen, her hands on her hips, and shook her head. "That's no trick. She wants the food, that's all. Come, Master Nicholas, and help me set the table."

The boy groaned and set down his fishing rod. Twinky seized the treat and fell over with it clasped in her paws.

"Missus," Florence said to Jane, "I've made spaghetti and meatballs. We can eat as soon as the spaghetti is ready."

"All right, Florence. Thanks."

Florence frowned sympathetically. "Would you like an aspirin, missus? Headache still bad?"

"I'll take some Tylenol in a minute. It'll pass."

Shaking her head, Florence returned to the kitchen. Jane heard Nick rattling around in the silverware drawer, then placing knives, forks, and spoons on the kitchen table.

From the kitchen also came the sound of Florence muttering to herself. "No excuse to put this off any longer. Better to get it out of sight."

Jane saw her cross in front of the doorway, carrying the cage they had used for Winky at the cat show.

"Florence, what are you doing?" Jane called.

"Finally cleaning this cage, missus. Dr. Singh said that if we don't want it, she'll take it and give it to a family who can use it. That's what I'll do, if you don't mind."

"No, I don't mind," Jane said, and got up from the sofa and wandered into the kitchen, where Nick was slipping napkins under the forks and Florence was removing the burgundy velvet curtain from inside the cage. Jane sat down at the kitchen table and put her head in her hands.

"Still hurt, Mom?"

"Mm."

"For goodness' sake," Florence said.

Jane looked up. "What is it?"

"The oddest thing, missus. There's something in the fold here."

Frowning, Jane got up to have a look. Florence was removing something from the hem of the curtain. She held it out in the palm of her hand for Jane to see. It looked like some sort of dried vegetation.

"What is it?" Nick asked.

Florence sniffed it. "Catnip!" She nodded, looking disgusted. "This," she said, "is why Winky was acting 'drunk' at the cat show—though she wasn't drunk at all. That horrid woman Gail must have dropped the catnip into the curtain's hem to put Winky out of the running."

"Why, that bitch!" Nick cried, and both women turned on him.

"Nicholas!" they reprimanded him in unison.

"You apologize this instant for using such language," Jane said.

"Sorry," he muttered. "But that's not fair."

"No, it's not," Jane agreed. "But in this world there are people who do things like that."

"Not drunk at all . . ." Nick repeated, shaking his head. At that moment Winky herself padded into the room and he scooped her up and hugged her until her eyes bulged.

Not drunk at all . . . Jane was lost in a memory of Tina Vale, slurring her words, stumbling in the Windmere's restaurant. Now Jane's headache was much worse, like an iron vise squeezing the sides of her head. She stumbled to the powder room off the foyer and slid open the medicine cabinet. In her haste to grab the Tylenol bottle she knocked the contents of the entire shelf into the sink.

"Oh, darn," she said, lowering her gaze.

And then she stood very still, staring down into the jumble of white plastic bottles and a few amber-colored plastic pill tubes.

She had left the powder room door open, and Florence appeared, looking concerned. "Are you all right, missus? I heard you drop something."

"I'm fine, Florence," she replied absently, "just fine."

For it was clear now, all of it.

She rushed to her study to make two telephone calls.

Chapter Eighteen

The following morning Jane pulled into a space in the parking lot behind her building, cut the engine, and sat for a moment, staring at the rear door to her office suite, thinking about the previous evening's epiphany. She checked her watch. It was only 8:40. Even dedicated Daniel wouldn't be in yet.

A dark form suddenly filled her window and she jumped, gasping.

It was Nat Barre. She smiled in surprise and got out. "You nearly gave me a heart attack."

"Sorry. I was waiting for you out front, and then I realized you'd be driving in here."

"Why were you waiting for me?"

"To say good-bye, and to thank you."

"Good-bye?"

He nodded sadly. "I'm going back to Green Bay. There's no reason for me to stay any longer. You and I both know Shelly's dead. She was the only reason I was here. I loved her, but she's gone, and nothing I can do will bring her back."

"Have you heard anything from the police?"

"They're looking for her ex-fiancé. Terry something."

"Ah, interesting."

He nodded. "Apparently he's got a history of violent behavior, even beat Shelly up a few times."

"How awful. Poor thing," she said, getting out. She took her briefcase from the passenger seat and shut the car door. "But what about your novel?"

"What about it? It seems more than likely that with Tina Vale gone, Corsair will publish it as originally planned. If not"—he shrugged, gave a quick smile—"I trust you to get me the best possible deal somewhere else."

She nodded understandingly. "When are you leaving?"

"My flight isn't until late this afternoon. Hey, it's a beautiful morning. Want to walk with me a little bit?"

"Of course." She opened the car door and put her briefcase back in. "I'll show you a nice place where we can walk."

She led him to the woods that edged the parking lot. "There's a path here," she said, starting into the dappled shadows. He crunched along behind her.

They walked silently, Jane in front. From the path they could see the backs of the shops on the green. Soon they had entered the thicker woods that bordered Plunkett Lane, which led to Hadley Pond.

They emerged onto Plunkett Lane, the narrow,

winding road through the thick woods, and continued walking. They passed the entrance to Hydrangea House on the right, and finally the road ended. Jane led Nat around some rocks and birches, and Hadley Pond came into view, beautiful in the sun, its stagnant surface abuzz with insects.

Right at the water's edge was a large boulder with a flattish top, and Jane leaned against it, gazing out over the water. Nat stood next to her, his gaze lowered thoughtfully.

"Nat," she said at last, "I've been wanting to thank you."

He looked up. "For what?"

"For being so understanding . . . for not blaming me for what Tina tried to do to your novel."

He was watching her. He was still for a long time. Then, "You know, don't you?" It was a statement, not a question.

"Yes," she replied calmly.

"About Tina?" he asked.

"And about Shelly."

He nodded resignedly, though she thought she caught the slightest hint of a smirk on his face. "In her suite at the Windmere, when I heard her plans to cancel my contract and realized she hadn't put them into motion yet, I knew she had to die. The question was, how?"

He laughed softly to himself. "Remember when I got so upset at the things she was saying and went to the bathroom? Well, I snooped in her medicine cabinet—everybody looks in other people's medicine cabinets—and then I had my answer."

She nodded, waited for him to continue.

"What I saw told me Tina had ALS—amyotrophic lateral sclerosis. It's often referred to as Lou Gehrig's disease. Do you know who Lou Gehrig was?"

"Of course I know. He was the Yankees' first baseman in the thirties."

"That's right. In thirty-nine his game started to decline. His reflexes were off. He stumbled and fumbled, and struggled to hit or catch the ball. No one understood what was going on. Some people thought he was drunk. But he wasn't. He had ALS.

"It's a progressive degenerative disease that attacks nerve cells in the brain and the spinal cord. Gradually, the brain loses its ability to control muscle movement. In the later stages of the disease, the victim becomes totally paralyzed, yet the mind remains totally unaffected. The victim is literally imprisoned in his or her own body.

"I'm a pharmacist—I know about these things. But I had to be sure. So I double-checked the medications in the *PDR* at the library here in town. Rilutek has been proven to be effective in prolonging ALS patients' survival. Not in curing them, just putting off the inevitable. Doctors also recommend high doses of vitamins E, C, and beta carotene. The Lioresal and Zanaflex are for stiffness and spasticity in the arms and legs. The Ultram is for pain relief. It couldn't have been clearer to me if there had been a sign on the mirror."

He gazed out over the pond, nodded slowly. "It made perfect sense, explained why Tina was slurring her words."

"I saw her stumble in the restaurant," Jane said, remembering.

"Exactly. Very much like a person who's had too much to drink. But she wasn't drunk. She was showing early symptoms of this terrible disease she was keeping a secret. I knew that once it was known that she had been suffering from ALS, no one would question her decision to commit suicide."

"And you made a note . . ."

"From the letter Tina had written, in which she said she was dropping *The Blue Palindrome.* I tore out the piece containing the words 'I can't go on.'

"I grabbed the key in the ashtray by the door as I rushed out. Right after lunch, I called the hotel's front desk on a house phone and pretended I was a letter carrier waiting in the lobby with a certified letter for Ian Stein. Then I called Tina's suite and said I was a courier with a package from New York for Ms. Vale, and would her assistant please come and get it. I waited behind a tree in the middle of the lobby and watched them come down. Then I slipped into the elevator, went up to the suite, and let myself in.

"Even then I had no idea how I was going to kill Tina. At first I thought she wasn't there. Then I heard water running and realized she was taking a bath. On my way to the bathroom I passed the dining room table and saw the toaster her husband had brought her that morning. That's when I knew what I was going to do to her. I grabbed it and went into the bathroom. She was soaking in soapsuds. She gasped when she saw me; she looked terrified. She screamed, but I knew she couldn't move—at least not quickly.

"There was an old-fashioned electrical outlet near the floor a few feet from the tub. I plugged in the toaster. She watched me. She demanded to know why I was in her suite, what I was doing, but from her eyes I could tell she knew. But there was nothing she could do about it. She made feeble movements with her arms, but she couldn't get out of the tub. She cried out for Ian and Shelly, but of course no one answered. I smiled and said, "Toast, bitch." Then I tossed the toaster into the bathtub.

"The lights dimmed and there was a bright flash and a shower of sparks and then smoke, a lot of it. And when it cleared, Tina was dead. She was all red, and she was staring at me, her head kind of crooked.

"I placed the 'suicide note' on the floor near the tub. Then I slipped back out of the suite—"

"Not realizing," Jane said, "that the missing key would destroy the whole illusion of suicide, despite the note's having been pronounced authentic."

He smiled. "It doesn't matter," he said happily. "She's dead now, no one will ever figure out who killed her, and I'll get paid."

She gazed at him through narrowed eyes, trying to understand. "And just to get that money—you killed her?"

"Sure," he said matter-of-factly. "She was nothing to me. From what I'd heard about her, I was doing the publishing industry a favor by getting rid of her. Besides, what she was going to do was completely unfair. She was going to punish me for something that had nothing to do with me, something between her and you. She hadn't even *read* my book. I had to keep it at Corsair. I knew St. Martin's wouldn't pay more than it had bid in the auction. In fact, it would probably have offered less. And it was highly doubtful that Hamilton Kiels and

Jack Layton would want the book. They would say no simply out of spite."

She gave him a grudging smile. "You know publishing quite well."

He continued as if he hadn't heard her, holding out his palms as if trying to get her to understand. "The near million dollars you got me from Corsair will make all the difference to me and Mother. I've already bought a house, a big house. I'm not about to lose it because of some female rivalry between you and Tina Vale.

"Tell me," he went on, "how'd you figure out I killed her?"

She inhaled the sweet summer air, thought back. "It was because of a comment my son's nanny, Florence, made about our cat Winky being 'drunk' on catnip. I realized that Tina wasn't drunk when we went to see her in her suite. She had a disease of some sort, but she had kept it such a deep, dark secret that no one knew about it . . . except her murderer, whose knowledge of her disease prompted him to create the suicide note.

"But Tina didn't commit suicide. Someone took that key from the ashtray by the door and came back to kill her. That person was the only person, other than Tina herself, who knew she was ill.

"Last night I dropped some pill bottles in the sink and it all came clear to me. You saw Tina's pills in her medicine cabinet when you went to the bathroom in her suite. I saw the same pills in Tina's condo."

He frowned. "You were in her condo?"

"Never mind that. All it took was a call to my doctor last night to find out that Rilutek is prescribed for ALS. Shelly had told me Tina had been seeing a therapist and a physical therapist. Now that made perfect sense."

He nodded. "That's right."

"But what about poor Shelly, Nat? Why did she have to die?"

"Who says I died?" Shelly stepped from the woods to the left of them.

Jane jumped.

"Sorry, Jane." Shelly approached them and took Nat's hand.

"Hello, darling," he said.

She kissed him on the lips, smiling. Then she turned to Jane and her smile disappeared and was replaced by a look of pure hatred. "You're the one who's going to die."

Chapter Nineteen

Jane stared at the young woman, flabbergasted. Speechless, she shook her head.

"Had you going there, didn't we?" Shelly looked at Nat lovingly. "He used a syringe to take some blood out of my arm. Then we splashed it all over the sofa and trashed my apartment. What a gas."

Finally Jane found her voice. "But why?"

"To get you to butt out," Shelly said. "We figured if you thought Tina's murderer had gotten me, too—not to mention the little present we left you—you'd be scared enough to mind your own business." She looked at Jane with pitying contempt. "I guess we were wrong."

"I was so worried about you . . ."

"Oh, can it. You were worried about *you! Your* career. *Your* reputation. You could have cared less about me." Shelly laughed. "Funny, isn't it? You thought my mother's murderer had killed me, and now we're going to kill you."

Jane said, "Did you kill your mother, Shelly?"

"No," Shelly replied impatiently, "Nat did. He just told you how. But afterward, after Nat and I had gotten together and I figured out what he'd done, I was glad."

"Glad? Why? Because she wasn't a good mother to you? Is that a reason to kill her?"

"Absolutely. I hated her frigging guts. Lets me come out to New York City—how generous! And when I get there she throws me a job as her flunky and stuffs me in a hovel on the Lower East Side, while she's living in Olympian House. Some mother, huh?"

She slid Nat an affectionate sidelong gaze. "I can't tell you how many times I would have loved to kill her—to just strangle the breath out of her while she was yelling at me to do something right or better—" Her voice broke and she began to cry. She sniffed, pulled herself together. "Then Nat had the balls to actually do it. And for that I'll love him forever."

Nat looked down modestly.

Jane asked Shelly, "How did you know Nat had killed your mother?"

Nat blushed. "After I slipped out of Tina's suite, I called the elevator—an idiotic thing to do, I now realize. I should have taken the stairs. At any rate, when the elevator door opened, there was Shelly in the elevator. She looked puzzled but didn't say anything. I panicked. I had to keep her out of the suite. So I asked if I could buy her a drink, and to my relief she accepted. Afterward, when she started to go back up to the suite, I convinced her to come up to my room—not difficult, since she was a bit drunk."

Shelly looked embarrassed.

"And we stayed in my room all afternoon." Nat took Shelly's hand and squeezed it tight. "Now I'm so glad." He paused.

Shelly said, "It wasn't until Thursday morning, when we were having breakfast at my apartment, that I got up the nerve to ask him why he'd been up on the penthouse floor that afternoon. There were only two suites on that floor. I didn't think he'd been visiting Dario. He must have been up there to see Mother, but why?"

"And I saw that she knew," Nat said. "It was so clear from her eyes—those beautiful green eyes . . ."

They gazed at each other lovingly.

Jane shook her head, confounded. "But why do *I* have to die?"

Shelly looked at her as if she were demented. "You don't see it, do you? *You* were the reason I had no father!"

Jane's gaze snapped to Shelly's face. "Then you know."

"Of course I know! Mother started telling me about it as soon as I was old enough to understand. Letter after letter she sent to me in Grand Rapids, telling me about how my dad wouldn't come back to her. She went to him when she was pregnant, after I was born, and several times after that. Later, when she was working with him at Silver and Payne, they even started up their affair again, but then you stole him away. He told Mother he loved *you*, that he had never consented to have a child with her and that I was her responsibility. What a guy, huh?"

"Shelly," Jane said, "it wasn't like that."

"How the hell do you know?" Shelly screamed. "Did he tell you about me? I don't think so. So how do you know? Tell me!"

"He *loved* me," Jane said pleadingly. "It wasn't that he hated you—he didn't even know you. And he never did love your mother. She should never have tried to use you to get him back."

Shelly blew out her breath in disgust and looked at Nat. "Can we kill her now? She is really getting on my nerves."

Nat looked down. For a moment the three of them were silent, as if waiting for something.

Suddenly Shelly looked up warily, her gaze darting to the woods behind Jane. "What was that?"

Jane spun around to look. Was it Stanley? She saw no one. She felt a sharp prick in the side of her neck, and flinched. "Ow!" She whirled back around.

"Made you look!" Shelly said, laughing.

Then Jane noticed the now-empty syringe in Nat's hand.

He smiled. "It's the best way," he said.

"The best way for what?"

"For you to die, of course."

Chapter Twenty

Nat gave Jane a frank look. "Let's be honest with ourselves, Jane. You have an unfortunate habit of solving murders. If I were to let you tell your detective friend you'd put this puzzle together, all my plans would be ruined."

"What did you inject me with?" Jane demanded. Shelly watched them both, eyes gleaming.

Nat gave a little chuckle. "It's not something I stock at the pharmacy, that's for sure. It's ketamine hydrochloride, or Special K. It's also known as Super K, Vitamin K, Kit Kat, Keller, Cat Valium, OK, Kid Rock, Make Her Mine . . . or just K. The date rape drug everybody's blabbing about. I'm sure you've heard of it."

"Yes," Jane said in a low voice. "I've heard of it."

"Except in this case," Nat said, "I have no intention of raping you. I'm just going to kill you."

Shelly giggled. As she did, her teeth began to drop from her face and the giggle became a high-pitched squeal. Then all the trees surrounding

Hadley Pond began to spin, as if it were all a big, wet merry-go-round, and she was swept along in a dizzying spin.

Jane's heart began to pound violently. Nausea rose in her throat. Then her arms and legs grew limp and she realized, somewhere outside herself, that she was lying prone on the ground beside the boulder.

Vaguely, not caring much, she felt strong arms pick her up like a baby and carry her into the pond. Water seeped into her shoes. The surface of the pond rose to meet her—it was cold, but she didn't mind—and she was sinking, the water pouring into her mouth and nostrils . . .

Then she was aware of the arms letting her go, of a confused churning in the water. She heard a man's deep voice shouting, a woman scream. She glanced to the side and saw two pairs of legs in trousers, moving quickly, as if the men they belonged to were struggling.

But it didn't matter. The world was slipping away. She saw other things now. Kenneth, smiling lovingly at her, telling her he hadn't meant to hurt her. Nicholas, laughing, running to her, throwing his arms around her in a tight hug. Stanley, putting his strong arm around her shoulders and pulling her to him for a gentle kiss. Handsome Daniel, looking up from his desk with that knowing smirk. Florence . . . Winky . . . her circle of friends, knitting on Louise's front porch.

She'd had a good life, full of people she loved and who loved her.

She relaxed, let the water take her.

Dying wasn't so bad, really.

Chapter Twenty-one

She opened her eyes, glanced about. She was in a bed, a hospital bed. High on the wall facing her was a television set, its screen dark. To the left was a large window that looked out on treetops bright in the sunshine.

A dark shape loomed into view. It was Stanley.

"Jane?" he said softly. "Are you with us?"

She smiled. "Of course I'm with you, silly. Where else would I be?"

He said nothing, but she could tell from his eyes that he had an answer he wasn't going to give her. "How do you feel?"

"Groggy? What's going on?" A soft pain blossomed in the front of her head. "Ooh. Why am I here? I've got this memory of water . . ."

He sat down carefully on the side of the bed. "Jane, you were at Hadley Pond. Do you remember?"

"Yes!" she said, eyes opening wide. "I do remember. I was with Nat and Shelly, those awful people, and Shelly distracted me—I thought she was seeing you—but it was so Nat could inject something into my neck."

"Actually," he said, "I was there."

"You were? Then why didn't you come?"

He laughed, shook his head. "You were supposed to slip your hand into your purse and dial my number on your cell phone, remember? You have it preprogrammed in. That's what we agreed on last night when you called me, do you remember that? You would wait for Nat in the parking lot behind your building. If he showed up—which we were pretty certain he would—I would follow the two of you at a distance. I would wait for your signal—I'd put my cell phone on vibrate—and move in quickly after you'd gotten Nat's confession."

He shook his head. "But when no signal came and time was passing, I started to get worried. I shortened the distance between us. And I got to the pond just as Nat injected you and carried you into the pond to drown you."

She could only stare at him in amazement.

"The doctor says the effects of the drug will wear off completely in another few hours. Apparently Nat didn't give you a lot—just enough to render you helpless. But this ketamine hydrochloride is a powerful drug. Veterinarians use it to tranquilize animals. Doctors used it during the Vietnam War as an anesthetic for battlefield surgery. You can see why it'll be a while before you're your old self again."

"Where are Nat and Shelly?"

"Safely locked away. Nat didn't struggle at all, but Shelly ran right across the pond and into the woods. Gave us quite a chase."

"Us?"

"I had to call for help. Fortunately, Dan Raymond was close by on Packer and came in less than a minute. He held onto Nat while I chased Shelly through the woods. I finally caught her, but would you believe she still gave me a wicked fight? Clawing and kicking, like a wild little tigress."

"I can believe it," she said. "She had two very willful parents."

He thought about that. "True."

There was a commotion out in the corridor. A nurse appeared in the doorway, her back to Jane and Stanley, arms outstretched to block the way. Just beyond her, Jane saw Nick and Florence.

"Wait!" the nurse said. "There's already someone in there. I'm not allowed to let in more than two at a time."

"Oh, nonsense," Florence said, flinging the nurse's arm aside and marching in, pulling Nick behind her by the wrist. "Missus!" she cried, hurrying up to Jane's bed. "Now what trouble have you gotten yourself into this time?"

Jane smiled weakly. "Just a little mishap in the water."

"Ha!" Florence gave her a knowing smile. "That's not what's going around town. You nearly got yourself murdered, that's what I heard."

The nurse still hovered in the doorway, an expression of consternation on her face. "Now only for a few minutes," she warned. Florence turned and gave her a deadly look. The nurse spun on her heel and trotted out in her white Birkenstock shoes.

"Mom!" Nick rushed up to stand near Jane's head. She took his hand and squeezed it tight.

"We had to see you, Mom," Nick said softly. "Had to make sure you were all right."

Into Jane's mind flashed the vision of Nick she had had before slipping into unconsciousness in Hadley Pond. Tears ran down her cheeks.

"Why are you crying, Mom?"

"Now, now, little mister," Florence said, moving closer to the bed and plunking down a large carpet bag. "More than two indeed!" she said, and opened the bag. Two furry heads popped out—Winky's orange-and-brown mottled one, and Twinky's in identical miniature.

"Florence!" Stanley cried. "You can't have them in here. This is a hospital. You're breaking every rule in the book."

"Oh, nonsense, Detective Greenberg," Florence said in her Trinidadian lilt, and gave him a toss of her hand. "This is a private room! Don't worry—no cat germs will get on any of the other patients."

"They wanted to come see you, too, Mom," Nick said with a huge smile.

Jane's tears had turned to tears of laughter. She reached out and petted the soft heads protruding from Florence's carpet bag. Twinky let out a tiny high-pitched mew. "Oh my goodness, I feel so much better already."

"And now you two had better get out of here before I arrest you," Stanley said with a look of mock sternness.

Florence gently pressed the two fuzzy heads back down into the bag and snapped it shut. "Not a problem. We're done. Good-bye, missus. Come home soon. I'm making my best sanoche for you."

"Yeah, hurry up, Mom."

They both kissed her on the cheek. Then they scurried out, laughing and talking.

Jane wiped the tears from her eyes. A wave of fatigue suddenly washed over her. "Oh, dear," she said on a yawn, "I feel so sleepy all of a sudden."

"Get some rest," Stanley said, gazing down at her with moisture in his own eyes. "We'll need you to testify at Nat and Shelly's trial."

"Is that all you need me for?" she asked groggily.

"You know it's not," he said and, leaning forward, gave her a long, tender kiss on the lips.

Epilogue

Three days later, Jane walked slowly along the path that cut across the village green. In her hand was the tall cup of iced coffee Ginny had given her at Whipped Cream as a welcome-back present. Stopping, she took a sip and looked around. A few feet to her left stood the brilliant white Victorian bandstand, its shadowy interior coolly inviting. She left the path, climbed the four wide steps, and sat down on the bench that ran around the inside.

It was a magnificent morning, the sky a dazzling blue, a warm, gentle breeze rustling the leaves of the oaks towering above the green and playing with Jane's hair.

But a deep sadness washed over her, and she felt a chill despite the warmth in the air.

One of her clients had tried to kill her. A writer she had believed in, fought for, had nearly killed her . . . for money.

Kenneth's daughter was twisted, mentally ill.

She, too, had plotted to kill Jane. She hoped Kenneth hadn't seen that. Now Shelly would no doubt go to prison. Kenneth's daughter . . . in prison.

With a deep sigh Jane rose from the bench and followed the path to Center Street. She stopped at the curb, looking at her office with its steeply pitched roof, faux gable, and half-timbers. Her gaze lighted on the brass plaque beside the front door: JANE STUART LITERARY AGENCY. To its right was a window; she saw Daniel pass in front of it.

With another sigh, she crossed Center Street and went in. Daniel, standing at the credenza at the back of the reception room, turned with a smile that quickly vanished. "Jane, what's wrong?"

She gave one shoulder a little shrug, forced a smile she didn't feel. "Guess I'm not quite myself yet."

He wet his lips, his expression concerned. "Maybe you're back too soon. Would you like me to drive you home so you can get some rest?"

"No, thanks, I'll be fine. Just have to get back into the swing of things."

He gave a tiny nod and she felt his gaze on her as she crossed to her office. Sitting down at her desk, she surveyed the massive heap of contracts, deal notes, manuscripts, and advance reading copies of books she'd sold. She looked away. She didn't have the heart for any of it.

As if from far away, she heard the phone ring at Daniel's desk, heard him answer it and put someone on hold.

"Jane?" came his voice tentatively from the intercom. "Are you taking calls?"

"Who is it?" she asked despondently.

"Salomé Sutton on one. I told her you were oc-

cupied—I didn't think you'd want to speak to anyone—but she insists. Should I say you've stepped
out?"

She checked her watch. It was 9:30, which
meant it was 6:30 in California. Salomé must really
need to talk to her. "No, that's okay. I'll take it."
She lifted the receiver. "Sal?"

"So where is it?" demanded Salomé's deep booming voice.

Jane frowned. "Where is what?"

Salomé groaned in exasperation. "My manuscript, what do you think? Did you send it to
Warner like I said? Where else is it?"

"Sal," Jane said patiently, "I don't even have the
termination letter from Corsair yet. We shouldn't
submit your manuscript until Corsair has actually—"

"Never mind that! I ain't getting any younger
here, and neither are you. You told me Corsair was
giving the book back. What else do you need to
know? I expect you to get it out there, Jane."

Jane shook her head, unable to suppress a little
smile. "All right, Sal, I understand how you feel.
I'll start submitting."

"Damn straight." Salomé paused, then said in a
softer voice, "Thanks, Jane."

Jane looked at the phone in surprise. "Why,
you're welcome, Sal."

"Let me know what happens, all right?"

"Will do," Jane said, put down the phone, and
looked up as Daniel's face peered around her
doorway.

"Sorry," he said, "but I've got Bertha on line
two. She insisted on holding, says it's vital that she
speak to you immediately."

"Heaven help me." Jane drummed her fingers on the desk. "Oh, all right, I'll take it."

"*Jane?*" came Bertha's shrieking voice. "Jane, you're not going to believe what that girl said to me."

"What girl?"

"Harriet!"

"Your editor? What did she say?"

"Well, I called her to discuss the cover of *Shady Lady*. I told her—in a very nice way, mind you—that I felt it . . . wasn't quite right, and she told me I'm a pain in the ass!"

Before Jane could stop herself, she barked out a laugh.

"Jane? Are you *laughing*?"

Jane coughed, cleared her throat. "A sneeze, Bertha, it was a sneeze. Now, what exactly did you say to Harriet?"

"I told you. That I didn't feel the cover was quite right."

"Come on, Bertha, what did you *really* say?"

There was silence on the line. Then Bertha said in a meek voice, "I told her the hero looked like Gumby."

"Like Gumby!"

"Well, he does, Jane. His hair is square and his face is that funny greenish color and he looks like Gumby to me. Jane, you have to step in and help me here. It's what I pay you for."

"I know what you pay me for, Bertha. Do me a favor and don't call Harriet for a while. I'll see what I can do."

"Thanks, Jane. You're one in a million," Bertha said, and hung up.

Brows raised in surprise, Jane put down the receiver. As she did, Daniel reappeared in the doorway. "I'm sorry to bother you again, but while you were talking to Bertha, Goddess called." He winced. "Says it's urgent."

"What is it with everybody today?" Jane said, and punched out Goddess's number in New York City.

"Jane, babe, you're gonna love it," Goddess said, chomping on gum.

"Love what?" Jane asked pleasantly.

"I've got an idea for my new book. You're gonna just *plotz.*"

Jane grinned. "All right, tell me what it is."

"Okay, okay. I'm gonna call it *Can You Stand It?* So can you guess what it's about?"

"*Can You Stand It?*" Jane frowned in puzzlement. "I give up."

"It's everything I hate!"

"Come again?"

"All the stuff in the world that I think sucks. You know, bumper stickers . . . wastebaskets . . . Daylight Saving Time. Isn't it a great idea?"

"Uh, let me think about it for a little while, all right, Goddess?"

"You don't love it," Goddess said flatly.

"No, no, I didn't say that. I just need to think about it."

"Okey-dokey." Chomp chomp. "Then call me." And she hung up.

Replacing the receiver, Jane laughed and shook her head. "*Can You Stand It?*" she repeated to herself.

"Pardon?" Daniel asked, having reappeared in the doorway.

"Goddess's new book. She wants to write about everything she hates."

His brows knit together and he wrinkled his nose. "Who would want to read that?"

She burst out laughing. "The same people who read her first book! Does it matter what she writes? She's Goddess!"

"That she is," he muttered, and wandered away.

Jane jumped up from her desk. She'd just remembered she promised Nick she'd buy him a new soccer goal at Sports Authority. She'd pop over to the Willowbrook Mall now, get it out of the way. The drive would do her good.

"I'll be back in about an hour," she told Daniel as she passed his desk. "In case anyone else calls."

"Too late." He smiled. "Stanley called while you were on with Goddess. Wants to take you to lunch. And Florence asked me to give you a message: Do you want callaloo or pelau for dinner? You're supposed to call her and let her know."

"Will do," she said, reaching for the door.

"Wait! What should I tell Stanley?"

"Tell him yes," she said, laughing. "I'll pick him up at twelve-thirty."

She headed down the back corridor toward the parking lot behind the building.

"Jane?" Daniel said, and she stopped and turned.

He looked up, kindness on his handsome face. "Welcome home."

"Thanks," she said, and gave him a brilliant smile. "It's good to be back."

Author's Note

Many readers have asked about Florence's Trinidadian cooking, looking for the recipes for some of her dishes. These two are sure to enhance your next "lime"—the Trinidadian expression for a fun time.

Florence's Stuffed Crab Shells

(4 servings)

2 tablespoons butter
4 cloves garlic, minced
4 tablespoons chopped onion
2 tablespoons minced parsley
2 tablespoons chopped green pepper
2 cups (500 milliliters) crabmeat
Pinch of salt
Pinch of pepper
Dash of hot pepper sauce
Dash of Worcestershire sauce

1 cup (250 milliliters) dry bread crumbs
4 cleaned crab backs/shells

In a large saucepan, melt butter. Add garlic, onion, parsley, and green pepper. Stir until soft. Add crabmeat, salt and pepper, and hot pepper sauce and simmer for 5 minutes. Add Worcestershire sauce and stir in bread crumbs. Remove pan from fire and combine mixture well. Divide mixture into four even portions and spoon into crab shells. Reheat in oven just before serving.

Serve with salad, rolls and butter.

Shrimp Salad with Rum

(4 servings)

This salad makes a wonderful summer party lunch. Cooked boneless chicken breast or lobster may be substituted for the shrimp. You may also use either canned pineapple chunks or fruit cocktail instead of the mandarin oranges.

1 pound (500 grams) cleaned, cooked shrimp
1 cup (500 milliliters) mayonnaise
¼ teaspoon salt
¼ teaspoon pepper
¼ teaspoon sugar
1 teaspoon tomato ketchup
1 teaspoon prepared mustard
½ teaspoon curry powder
Few drops lemon juice
1 tablespoon rum
1 cup (250 grams) canned mandarin orange segments, drained

2 tablespoons canned sliced mushrooms, drained
4 large lettuce leaves
4 lemon wedges

In a bowl combine all ingredients except lettuce leaves and lemon wedges. Line four plates with lettuce leaves. Divide shrimp mixture into four even portions and spoon onto lettuce leaves. Garnish each plate with a lemon wedge.

I love hearing from my readers. If you have a comment about *Toasting Tina* or any of my books, I invite you to e-mail me at evanmarshall@The Novelist.com, or write to me at Six Tristam Place, Pine Brook, NJ 07058-9445. I always respond to reader mail. For a free bookmark, please send a self-addressed stamped envelope. And please visit my Web site at http://www.TheNovelist.com.

—Evan Marshall

Please turn the page for an exciting sneak
peek at Evan Marshall's next
Jane Stuart and Winky mystery
CRUSHING CRYSTAL,
coming next month in hardcover!

Everyone watched Myrtle step out from behind the table and march up behind Crystal, who seemed unaware of the other woman's presence.

"I want to talk to you," Myrtle said in a loud, menacing voice.

Crystal started and spun around. "What—?"

Myrtle stepped closer to Crystal so that there was barely a foot between their faces.

"I want you to take back what you said to DYFS," Myrtle demanded in a loud voice. "Call them. Say it was a mistake."

Crystal's eyes widened for the briefest moment, then narrowed to slits. Her nostrils flared. "No." She drew out the word, as if savoring it.

Myrtle's mouth opened slightly, but nothing came out. Then, slowly, her lips drew together. "You horrible, horrible woman," she said in a low voice. "Sticking your nose into other people's business . . . thinking you know everything . . . ruining people's lives . . ."

Then she clamped her mouth shut. Suddenly she spun around, her bag swinging wide, and marched into the library's rear room.

Jane looked around the table. All eyes were still on Crystal, who had already turned back to what she'd been doing and looked as if nothing untoward had taken place.

"Now then," Mindy said in a high squeaky voice, and cleared her throat.

Jane realized Ginny was looking at her. Jane gave her a little shrug and returned her attention to Mindy, who was looking across Myrtle's now-empty place at Gabrielle in the next chair, asking her a question. ". . . if Uncle Ned had been in the barn?"

Gabrielle stared at her. "Huh?"

The meeting continued pretty much that way—Mindy cheerfully asking questions about *River to Yesterday,* no one really listening except Penny, who sat attentively, offering answers when no one else would.

Suddenly Gabrielle stood up. "Excuse me," she said in her deep voice. "Need some water." With a little smile, she left the table and went into the library's rear room, presumably to get a drink from the water fountain outside the restrooms.

While she was gone, Jane managed to answer a question about the novel under discussion, since she had, after all, read it. As she finished her remarks, Gabrielle returned from the back room, with Myrtle close behind her. Gabrielle returned to her seat at the table, while Myrtle marched past them all and out the building's front doors.

Ginny leaned close to Jane. "Things ought to be

a bit calmer now," she whispered, when at that moment one of the library's front doors opened again and a man walked in. He was young—in his twenties—and quite handsome, with regular features and neatly trimmed brown hair. On his back was a worn green backpack.

He stopped in front of the doors and slowly scanned the library. Simultaneously, Crystal returned to the central area where he was standing. She gave him a polite smile and swept past him.

"You—" he said, and she stopped and stared at him. "Are you Crystal Ryerson?"

She frowned. "Yes . . ."

"You monster!" he cried into her face.

"I beg your pardon?" she said, placing her hands on her ample hips. She tossed her head and glared down her nose at him. "Who *are* you?"

"How dare you go to my boss and tell her I'm a thief! You didn't even see me with that computer. Who told you about it?"

Crystal made no reply, only gazed impassively into his reddening face.

"I don't believe this," Doris said.

So this, Jane gathered, was Mr. Stanton from Nick's school. She remembered her telephone conversation with Crystal the previous Thursday night.

"I hope you didn't say anything about Mr. Stanton."

"Mr. Stanton?"

"Yes, you remember. With the computer in his car?"

"Oh, him! No, of course not."

Jane should have known.

Ginny nudged her with her elbow. "Who *is* he?" she whispered.

Jane gave a quick shake of her head to indicate she didn't want to talk now.

"If you must know—not that it's any of your damn business . . ." Stanton railed, "I was taking that computer home to fix it."

"Were you?" Crystal asked skeptically.

He shook his head as if he couldn't believe someone like Crystal could exist. "You have no idea what you've done to me. It took me nearly a year to find this job. I can't afford to lose it. I've got a wife and a baby at home. Please—tell Nina you made a mistake."

Crystal took a deep breath through her nose and tossed her head. "No."

"Unbelievable," he said, shaking his head again. "You're despicable, do you know that? You've ruined my life."

He turned and stomped past her, into the library's rear room.

Jane looked around the table. All eyes were wide and fixed on Crystal, who remained in the middle of the floor. Gabrielle's eyes were slits, and she slowly turned her head from side to side.

After a moment, Crystal gathered herself together and resumed her walk across the room, positioning herself at the checkout desk and calmly checking in books from the return slot.

Mindy cleared her throat. "Well," she began uncertainly, "I suppose we should—"

"We should give it up," Doris intoned from the other end of the table.

"Doris!" Rhoda said in surprise.

Doris threw out her hands. "The book stinks, everybody seems to have something else to talk about—what's the point?"

Mindy looked down, deeply disappointed.

"*I* would like to continue the meeting," Jane said, feeling sorry for Mindy.

"Me, too," Ginny said.

"All right, then." Mindy gave a wan smile, looking vaguely encouraged. "Why don't we—"

At that moment Stanton reappeared from the back room. His gaze fixed in front of him, he stomped back across the floor to the front entrance and went out. Jane glanced across the room. Behind the checkout desk, Crystal appeared to have taken no notice.

"Now then," Mindy tried yet again, "where were we?"

Doris said, "We were talking about what would have happened if Uncle Ned had been in the barn." She sounded unutterably bored.

"Right," Mindy said cheerfully. "Thank you. Any ideas?"

Penny raised her hand. "Then Agnes would have been able to tell him what had happened to her, and he might have helped her."

"Interesting," Mindy said, slowly nodding. "Good, Penny." She frowned, concentrating, then looked up at Jane and laughed. "Talking about the barn reminded me of the book I wanted to recommend to you. It's *Down on the Farm,* by . . . Oh, dear, I can't seem to recall the author's name."

From across the room, Crystal piped up, "Hodges. Lauren Hodges."

Mindy tossed her an uneasy look. "Right," she called. "Thank you. Jane, remind me to get it for you before you leave."

"I'll get it," Crystal said pleasantly. She came out

from behind the checkout desk and walked into the rear room.

"Any other ideas?" Mindy asked the group.

"I'm cold," Doris said.

"Yes, it is chilly in here," Louise agreed.

Mindy nodded. "We've been having trouble with the heat. I've asked Rich to fix it, or to call in whoever needs to fix it, but I don't know where he is with that. For that matter, I don't know where he is!"

"Who's Rich?" Jane asked.

"Rich Weldon," Mindy replied, surprised. "He's the custodian. You know Rich."

"Yes," Jane said, vaguely remembering him.

"He never showed up for work today," Mindy continued.

"Here, Doris," Louise said, removing her cardigan. "Put this on."

"Thanks," Doris said, taking it.

At that moment a woman's high-pitched scream pierced the air, followed by a terrible crash. Everyone froze.

The sounds had come from the back room of the library.

"Dear Lord," Mindy said in a whisper, jumped up, and ran toward the back, the other women close behind her. Together they scrambled into the back room . . . and gasped at what they saw.

An entire wooden floor-to-ceiling bookcase had collapsed. It lay twisted atop a mountain of books—and atop Crystal, whose head lay directly under the bookcase's topmost shelf. Blood ran from a gash at the side of her head.

Jane hurried forward, heart pounding, and picked her way through the books. She bent down and tried to lift the bookcase, but it was no use. The old wood was so heavy she couldn't move it an inch.

"Crystal," she said softly, leaning close, and now she could see her face—its expression frozen, the brown eyes wide with fear.

Mindy took a step toward Jane and said in a low voice, "Is she—"

"Yes," Jane said, "I'm afraid so."

Rhoda came forward. "But how—?" she said to Jane.

Jane looked up at the wall against which the bookcase had stood. About eight feet up were two heavy metal L-brackets, about a foot apart. The vertical segments of these brackets appeared bolted firmly to the wall. The horizontal segments stuck straight out into the air.

Mindy was studying them. "They were bolted to the bookcase. It's as if they just . . . let go."

"What are you doing?" came Doris's brisk voice, and Mindy and Jane turned to her. "Get ahold of yourselves. A woman has been killed. Call the police."

"Yes," Mindy said with a haunted look. "We should, Jane." Her eyes widened slightly. "Call your boyfriend, Stanley."

"Yes," Jane said. Stanley would know what to do. She ran to the front room and went behind the checkout desk to make the call. As she dialed, she had a horrible thought. She put her hand to her mouth, suddenly feeling so hot she thought she might faint.

How would she tell Florence?

Jane stood on the path that led up to the library's entrance and watched Stanley emerge from the building. Mindy, who had been waiting at the foot of the steps, hurried up to him. As she spoke to him, she had to put her head way back, for although he was of medium height, he was easily a head taller than she. He wore a blue blazer over gray flannel slacks—he'd come out without his coat again, Jane noted. He had such a sweet, concerned look in his dark brown eyes as he listened to Mindy. A wind had come up. It played with his straight sandy hair, which usually remained neatly in place on his forehead.

Abruptly he gave Mindy a vigorous nod, pressed her upper arm reassuringly, then descended the stairs and walked down the path to where Jane waited.

She'd have kissed him hello if there weren't so many people around—police officers standing at the edge of the library lawn, several of them watching Stanley.

"Are you all right?" he asked her.

She nodded. Suddenly she felt her face contort, and tears sprang to her eyes. "It's so awful, Stanley. I know I said mean things about her, but I—I never—"

"I know." Nodding, he put his arm around her and pulled him to her, clearly unconcerned about who might be watching. "You mustn't feel guilty."

She sniffed hard. "It was so horrible. The whole bookcase— How could such a thing happen?"

Stanley's expression underwent an odd transformation. He was watching her, as if trying to read her the right way. At last he said, "Come to my car."

She frowned. "What?"

He motioned with his hand for her to walk with him. They got into his squad car parked at the far left edge of the library lawn, near the town hall.

"What's going on?" she asked him.

"Jane, I'm going to tell you this because you'll hear it anyway, and I want it to come from me."

She lowered her brows in confusion. "Hear what from you? What is it?"

"Jane, it looks as if Crystal . . . Well, it seems pretty clear that what happened in there wasn't an accident."

"What?" She gave her head a few quick shakes. "Stanley, what are you talking about? The bolts came loose. The bookcase fell on her."

"Yes, the bookcase fell on her, but the bolts didn't *come loose*. They were *removed*."

For a moment she just stared at him, the meaning of what he'd said sinking in. "Removed?" she whispered. "Someone took them out?"

"Yes."

"But why?"

He took a deep breath, considering. "Someone wanted the bookcase to fall."

"On Crystal?"

"It appears so."

"How can you be so sure?"

He looked at her. "Because they're gone."

A movement caught her eye and she looked up. Two men carrying a stretcher had emerged from the library's front doors. A sheet covered Crystal's large body. Carefully the two men descended the wide stairs and moved toward an ambulance Jane now noticed parked a few cars ahead of Stanley's car.

Suddenly she turned to him. "I've got to get home. I've got to tell Florence before someone else does."

* * *

"Oh, missus!" Florence wailed, embracing Jane fiercely.

Jane patted her back. She began to cry. "I know. I know. It's horrible. I'm so sorry."

Suddenly Florence drew back and looked Jane in the eye. "Yes, it's horrible, and it's my fault."

"What!"

"Yes. I was the one who told my sister she should come up here and interview for that job at the library. If I had only minded my own business, she would be alive now." Shaking her head miserably, Florence dropped into a kitchen chair. She looked up at Jane imploringly. "But who would have wanted to kill her?"

Was she serious? "Well . . ."

"Oh, I know what you're going to say. She was meddlesome and bossy and some people didn't get along with her. But she had a good heart, missus, she really did. You have no idea how good she was to me when we were growing up in Trinidad. With so many children, my mother was always busy. It was Crystal who raised me, really." She paused, a thought occurring to her. "Thank God our mother isn't alive to know about this."

"Why are you guys crying?"

Nick had appeared in the doorway, Twinky in his arms. Alphonse appeared behind him, padded into the kitchen, and began walking around Jane, pressing himself against her legs. He would have to be walked.

Jane went up to Nick and put her hand on his upper arm. "Honey, something very sad has happened. Florence's sister Crystal . . . well, she died."

Nick's eyes grew wide. "She died?"

Florence nodded. "Yes, Nicholas." She lowered her head and started to cry again.

Nick walked slowly over to her and gave her a hug. Florence hugged him back tightly. "Thank you," she said through her tears. Then she released him, sniffed hard, and stood. "I'd better start getting dinner ready. And Stanley—he'll want to speak to me, won't he, missus?"

"Yes," Jane replied. "You're her next of kin."

"I am," Florence said, turning to the counter, where she had set out carrots and onions for chopping. "I am."

A whistling wind rattled the windows of Jane's study. Gazing out into the darkness, Florence hugged herself for warmth. Then she turned to face Jane, who sat a few feet away. "It makes no sense, missus."

Jane smiled gently. "But I've told you exactly what happened."

"No, I know that. I understand everything that happened up until my sister died. What I don't understand is *why*? Why would anyone want to kill poor Crystal?"

Was it possible, Jane wondered, that Florence really couldn't see what kind of person her sister had been? Florence had apologized numerous times for Crystal's behavior, which meant she must have been aware of how people perceived her. But Jane would not remind Florence of any of this.

Jane frowned, gathering her thoughts. Finally she said slowly, "Who's to say how people will react to another person . . . to something another person has done? Maybe someone was angry at your sister—"

"And *killed* her?" Florence's dark eyes were immense. "Out of anger?"

"It's been known to happen."

Florence cast her gaze down at the floor, pondering this concept. Then sharply she looked up, her face full of resolve. "You have to help me."

"Help you?"

"Yes. You have to help me find out who did this to my poor sister."

"Oh, Florence . . ." Jane began, shaking her head.

"You know how to do it, missus. You've done it before. Please." Florence's eyes searched Jane's. "I'm not stupid. I know what Crystal was. She was bossy and self-righteous, a know-it-all, and she could be a terrible schemer. I know all that. But she didn't deserve to die. I loved her. Please. Help me find out who did this."

"But the police—"

"Pfoosh!" Florence made a sound of disgust and turned her head away. "No offense to your Stanley, missus—you know I love him dearly—but the police here, they are a bunch of bungling idiots! What have they done in the past when someone has been killed? No help at all! It was *you* who figured out what happened to poor Marlene. *You* who found out who that poor girl behind Hydrangea House was. *You* who caught the person who killed Mr. Kenneth's cousin Stephanie. Then there was your poor friend Ivy, and only three months ago, Tina Vale—"

"Okay, okay. Maybe I've been lucky."

"Lucky! Don't sell yourself short, missus. Luck

had nothing to do with it. You have a way of putting the pieces together. And I need you to help me put *these* pieces together for Crystal." Florence leaned toward Jane, wringing her hands. "Will you do that?"

"I . . ." Jane hesitated. Then she let her shoulders drop. "Yes, of course I will."

"Thank you, missus. Thank you." Florence gazed out again into the darkness. A branch whipped by the wind tapped the window glass. Tears came to her eyes. "She's out there, lying in a cold room, all alone. My sister who ran on the beach with me at Chacacabana, who taught me how to cook . . ." She laughed through the tears. "Who poured a bucket of water on my head when I wouldn't eat my vegetables . . . No, missus," she said, turning back to Jane, "my sister did not deserve to die."

Grab These
Kensington Mysteries

Mischief, Murder &
Mayhem – Grab These
Kensington Mysteries

More Mischief, Murder
& Mayhem in These
Kensington Mysteries